SUGAR CREEK GANG

LOST
IN THE BLIZZARD

SUGAR CREEK GANG

LOST
IN THE BLIZZARD

Original title:
Lost in a Sugar Creek Blizzard

Paul Hutchens

MOODY PRESS • CHICAGO

Copyright, 1950, by
PAUL HUTCHENS

Moody Press Edition. 1965

ISBN 0-8024-4817-8

25 27 29 30 28 26

Printed in the United States of America

1

THE FIRST time I saw that great big dangerous-looking snake, it almost half scared me to death — the way it flattened out its ugly head, with its fierce-looking, shovel-shaped nose, and also the way its neck expanded at the same time until it was almost three times as big as it had been.

It was making a hissing sound like air being let out of a tire of my blue and white bicycle.

I stopped stock still and stared at it, my whole body tense with fright. It was lying in a half coil and had been sunning itself in the sandy path that leads from the two big pig-nut trees above our garden to an old iron pitcher pump at the other side of Pop's farm.

Say, if anybody had seen me staring at that savage-looking, *mad-looking and mad-acting,* reddish-yellow, thick-bodied snake with the irregular-shaped blotches of brownish-black scattered all the way down its length from its neck to its tail, he'd have said my eyes had widened out until they were as big as the puffed-out head and neck of that snake. I was barefoot, too, so if the snake had wanted to, it could have bit my foot or my ankle or one of my ten bare toes — I was that close to him. I didn't even have a stick in my hand like I sometimes have when I walk around our farm, so I couldn't sock the snake like a boy likes to do when he sees one.

"Hiss-s-s-s-s-s-sss!" the big-bodied snake said to me fiercely.

Its ugly head was shaped like a triangle in our arithmetic book in school and its nose was turned up at the tip like it was trying to smell to see what kind of strange animal I was, myself.

As I said, I was scared stiff. My greenish-gray eyes must have been bulging out of their sockets almost, and I was wondering what on earth to do to kill the snake. If I tried to jump back, would it make a lunge for me and strike me with its fangs? I couldn't help but think of one of the members of the Sugar Creek Gang whose name is Dragonfly, and who, when he sees something exciting before the rest of us do, always hisses like a snake, and his own eyes get big and round like a dragonfly's eyes are all the time, which is why we called him by that name.

Well, not having a stick to sock the snake, and not knowing what else to do, and being scared anyway, I let out several screams. In fact, I had already screamed maybe a half dozen times, on account of the snake was not only puffing out its neck, and hissing, but its triangle-shaped head was darting in and out in my direction very fiercely.

I must have come to quick life all of a sudden, 'cause the next thing I knew, I had leaped back about six feet and was looking all around for a rock to sock the snake with, but I couldn't find any on acount of Pop and I had been picking up all the rocks from our farm for years and taking them out of the fields so we could raise better crops.

Even though I didn't find any rock, I did spy a big clod of dirt almost as big as my baby sister's Charlotte Ann's pretty round head, so I quick stooped, grabbed it up in my kinda-big-for-a-boy's hands, lifted it high over my head, and with all my fierce, half scared, half mad strength, hurled it down toward the snake's shovel-shaped snout.

But as much as I hate to have to admit it, I missed him and the dirt clod squished itself into a million particles of dirt and dust right beside where the snake's head had been a second before the clod got there.

And then, the queerest thing I ever saw happened. That big forty-inch-long, heavy-bodied, yellowish-red snake all of a sudden opened its mouth wide and began to twist itself into and out of several kinds of knots like I had actually hit it, and injured it terribly; and the next thing I knew, it gave itself a sidewise flip-flop and landed on its back with the prettiest yellowish-green snake's stomach I ever saw exposed to the hot sun, which was shining down on both of us.

Say, the second he got on his back with his very pretty yellowish-green stomach exposed, he all of a sudden quit wriggling and twisting, and just lay there like he was absolutely dead.

What on earth! I thought. I must have hit him after all! And yet I knew I hadn't 'cause

I'd seen my clod of dirt miss him almost six inches. All that had happened to him was maybe a lot of dust and dirt had spattered him in the eyes and onto the side of his mad head and his big three-inch-wide puffed-out neck. But there he lay, not making a move and looking like a terribly big fishing worm that was as lifeless as a fishing worm is when a robin has pecked it to death, just before feeding it to one of her babies.

Well, what do you know? I thought. I *scared* him to death! I didn't know if it was my clod of dirt, or the way I had yelled at him. But, of course, he couldn't actually be dead. I looked around and saw a long stick which I hadn't seen before, and just to make sure, I picked up the stick, and poked at the snake, and it didn't even move the end of its tail, but lay absolutely quiet.

I don't know what made me do what I did just then, but I all of a sudden felt very brave, kinda like maybe David must have felt in the Bible story, when he had killed a great big giant with one little stone out of his slingshot. I remembered that David was supposed to have had red hair, like I had, so I looked down at that giant shovel-nosed snake, and yelled down at it, "Get up, you coward! Get up and fight like a man!" Having the long stick in my hand, I knew I could kill him, like I had a lot of garter snakes and water snakes around Sugar Creek.

So I yelled at him again, calling him a coward to let a ten-year-old boy scare him to death, and then I got another surprise. From the direction of the iron pitcher pump, which is right close by a stile which we go over to go to school in the fall and winter and spring, I heard a boy's yell, and I knew it was the voice of my friend, Poetry, the barrel-shaped member of our gang who was my almost best friend, and whose house I was on my way over to when I had run onto the snake.

. . . *"Who*'s a coward?" Poetry yelled to me from the top of the stile where he was when I looked up and saw him. Then he scrambled his fat self down the stile's four steps and came puffing toward me, walking up the dusty path, which, as I told you, runs from two big tall pignut trees at the end of our garden, across the field I was in, clear down a little hill to the stile.

"I just killed a great big snake," I said, "a fierce-looking one about six feet long and as big around as your wrist," — only it wasn't quite that big, but now that I was a hero, it seemed like the snake was bigger than it was — and besides I wanted Poetry to *think* it was, until he got to where he could see it himself, then I'd tell him I was only fooling, which different members of the gang were always doing to each other anyway.

I stood there, looking at Poetry lumbering toward me. Also, I kept glancing at my defeated enemy, wondering how on earth I'd managed to scare it to death.

In a jiffy, Poetry was there, with both of us looking down at the yellowish-green, upturned stomach of the snake, both of us standing back about eight or ten feet from it.

"How'd you do it?" Poetry asked. "What'd you hit him with — that stick?"

"I *scared* him to death!"

"*Scared* him to death! That's just plain dumb. You can't do that to a snake. You have to hit him with something."

"I did," I said with a mischievous grin in my mind. "I threw my voice at him, and it hit him, and he just twisted himself up into a couple of knots, like a boy does when he gets the cramps from eating green apples, and plopped himself over on his back and died, right in front of my eyes. I'm a ventriloquist. I can throw my voice, you know."

Well, it was fun kidding Poetry. Then I told him I'd missed the snake with a clod of dirt, but that he'd died anyway.

"Maybe there was a rock in the clod," Poetry said, "and when the clod hit the ground six inches from his head, and burst in pieces, the rock flew out and hit him on the head, and it just sort of accidently killed him."

That reminded me of red-haired David's one small smooth stone that had killed a terribly big giant. If there was anything in the world I'd rather do than anything else, it was to imagine myself to be somebody else — like a hero in our history books at school or a brave character in the Bible. Right that second, I remembered David's one small smooth stone had socked Giant Goliath, killing him deader than a doornail. David had rushed up to the fallen giant and had stood on him with his feet; and it seemed like maybe I ought to do that to my giant-sized, shovel-nosed snake. "That's Giant Goliath," I said to Poetry, "and I'm David. I'm going to stand on him and cut off his head and —"

"STOP!" Poetry said, "He might NOT be dead. Here, give me that stick."

He took my stick, eased himself up closer to the snake, and poked at it, but it didn't move at all, not even its tail.

"It's dead, all right," I said, feeling even prouder of myself than I had been, because of what I had done.

Right that second, Poetry looked at his wrist watch and frowned at it and said, "Hey, we've got to get going! There's a gang meeting down at the spring. Big Jim just phoned our house, and it's very important. He tried to call you but nobody answered your phone, so I was on my way over to get you."

2

I FORGOT to tell you that my folks had gone to town, and they had told me I could go over to Poetry's house that afternoon just as soon as I had finished hoeing a few rows of potatoes. Pop hadn't said how many rows, so I asked him, and he said, "Let your conscience be your guide. But there are several that ought to be done."

My conscience wasn't sure how to be a guide to a boy that didn't like to hoe potatoes. so I thought I ought to know exactly how many "several" was and maybe that would help. As soon as Pop and Mom and Charlotte Ann had gone, I looked up the word in our brand-new dictionary, and it said, "indefinite: more than one or two, but not many." The only thing was, I forgot and left the dictionary open right where I had been looking, and when Pop came home later, he found out what I had done and — but that's getting ahead of the story.

Anyway, just to be sure I'd hoed *several*, I actually hoed *three*, which was more than one or two, but wasn't many.

Then I had left my hoe in the shade, leaning it up against one of the big pignut trees at the end of the garden, and had started down the dusty path toward the stile, over which I was going to climb and then hurry as fast as I could to Poetry's house. That's when I had run onto the snake in that dry sunny path.

Whenever Big Jim called a meeting, and wanted it in a hurry, we all tried to get there as quick as we could; so when Poetry told me about the gang meeting, we decided to go right away.

"What kind of a snake is it?" Poetry said, and I said, "I don't know, but maybe Pop will know. He knows pretty near everything there is to know about snakes and birds and toads and fish and things."

"My Pop does too," Poetry said, and even though I knew that my Pop knew more than Poetry's Pop any day, I didn't say so, but we started to go back up the path toward the pignut trees and our garden. In a little while we'd be going past our house with its big green ivy-vine that covers nearly all the south side — with just a little open space upstairs where my bedroom window is — and also past another iron pitcher pump at the end of a board walk about twenty feet from our back door, then we'd go on past the mailbox at the side of the road, that says on it "Theodore Collins," which is my Pop's name, then we'd swish across that dusty, gravelled road, vault over a rail fence, and, once in the woods, we'd start running; and quicker'n a jack rabbit could do it, we'd be at the spring where the gang was going to meet.

Poetry, being as sure as I was that the snake was dead, did what lots of boys do to dead snakes, picked it up by the tail and dragged it along behind him till we got to the pignut tree. There he draped it over a rail fence at the edge of our garden and we left it there, till Pop should get home in the late afternoon when I was going to show it to him and ask him what kind of a snake a boy could scare to death with just his voice, or by missing him with a big clod of dirt.

We stopped to look at the snake a jiffy,

hanging there with his head on one side and his tail on the other, and he really looked BIG — almost as long as Little Jim is tall — little Jim being the littlest member of the Sugar Creek Gang, a swell guy with pretty brown curls on the top of his round head, and blue eyes, and a very serious face — also sometimes his face was mischievous.

All of a sudden Poetry looked at our garden and said, "You been hoeing potatoes this afternoon?"

"Sure," I said, half proud of myself.

"It's hard to believe," Poetry said and ducked to get out of the way of my flying fist, which I wouldn't have hit him hard with, he being my almost best friend.

"Well, I'm surprised," he said, but it wasn't funny and I wouldn't laugh.

Just that second, there was a heavy clumsy movement at my feet. Looking down, I saw a big fat friendly-looking garden toad which I had almost stepped on and smashed.

"Hi, Warty," I said down to him.

"Hi, *who?*" Poetry exclaimed.

"Warty," I said, "Pop's pet toad. He lives here in the garden and eats cutworms and mos-

quitoes and bugs and stuff. Last night Pop and
I made a big supper for him."

"Supper! For a *toad!*" Poetry looked down
at Warty, who was sitting as quiet as an old
setting hen on a nest, and all widened out like
a mother hen covering a nest full of eggs.

"Sure," I said, and explained, "Pop hung
a sheet over the fence right here, right close
to where Warty hangs out, and turned his big
electric lantern on the sheet for fifteen minutes, and all kinds of bugs and night moths
and things flew against it, and those that
plopped down to the ground, Warty gobbled up.
Look, he's as fat as a stuffed toad today," —
which Warty was. I'd never seen him so fat in
my life. When I was littler, Pop had taught
me to be very glad if we had a toad living in
our garden 'cause toads are the farmer's
friends. "A toad will eat over ten thousand in-
jurious insects in one summer," Pop had told
me.

"Let's see you throw your voice at *him*, and
kill *him*," Poetry said. But I wouldn't. Besides, I thought Poetry was just making fun
of me. So he decided to try it himself, which
he did, yelling down at Warty in his half-man-

half-boy's voice, which is the kind of voice he had, he being at the age in his life when a boy is part boy and part man, like a tadpole about to turn into a frog.

But Warty, who had dived halfway under a rhubarb leaf, just blinked his lazy-looking eyes at us or at nothing and didn't move a muscle.

Well, we had to hurry on. Just as we reached our hen house, I turned around to take a final look at the big fierce-looking snake hanging on the garden fence, but say! he wasn't there!

Poetry looked at the same time, and said, "Your dead snake doesn't like hanging on a fence in the hot sun for people to look at, or else he lost his balance and fell off," which was probably right, I thought. Anyway when Pop came home, I could remember where the snake had been hanging, and it'd be as easy as falling off a rail fence to find it lying there in the weeds.

"What's that song you're whistling?" Poetry asked me all of a sudden.

"What song?" I listened to my thoughts in a jiffy, and, sure enough, I had been whistling a song and didn't know it. In a second I remembered what it was, and it was one of the hymns we sometimes sing in the Sugar Creek Church on Sunday mornings when Mom and Pop and Charlotte Ann and I are all sitting together in a row. I could hardly believe my astonished thoughts when I realized that it was a song called "A Mighty Fortress," which I remembered was written by a man who, our minister said, was a converted priest named Martin Luther; and the place in the song that I had been whistling was where it tells about Satan, and the words were, "One little word shall fell him."

I didn't understand it very well, but I could sort of feel that it was the Saviour of the world whose word was really strong enough to hit the Devil and knock the living daylights out of him — even if He threw at him only one little word.

Anyway I felt kind of good inside for some reason.

But it was time to get going to the gang meeting. "I wonder what Big Jim wants a meeting for?" I asked Poetry as we decided to run to make up the lost time.

Boy oh, boy, if I had known what that gang meeting was going to be about, and also what was going to happen to us before the things we had planned at that meeting were finally all finished, I'd *really* have been excited. If I had known how, later that year, when the summer was over and winter came, and there was a lot of snow everywhere and the gang had to make a very important trip up into the hills to the old haunted house I told you about in the last story of the Sugar Creek Gang, — *boy!* if I had only known! But I didn't, so Poetry and I weren't even excited as we hurried on to the spring where we were to meet the gang.

Say, I can hardly wait till I write that far before telling you about that terribly exciting experience. If we hadn't had Big Jim's rifle along with us, every one of us might have died.

3

EVEN WHILE POETRY AND I were running lickety-sizzle through the woods, following the path made by barefoot boys' bare feet, wondering what on earth could be so important that Big Jim, our leader, had to call a special meeting to tell us about it, I was still thinking about that big heavy-bodied, four-foot-long snake I had killed all by myself, either by scaring it to death or maybe by a small stone that had been in the clod of dirt I had missed him with.

Pop would be proud of me, I thought, for killing such a big snake, but my grayish-brown-haired Mom would probably look at me across the supper table and say, "Let me see your hands. Are you sure you washed them after handling that snake?" — which is the same kind of question Mom asks me after I've handled almost anything, especially if she wants me to help her with some work in the house, which Little Jim says his Mom also asks him maybe twenty times a day.

Poetry, who was puffing along behind me, all of a sudden yelled a breathy yell at me and said, "Hey! The papaws are turning brown! Look!"

I stopped half quick, looked to the right to the thicket of papaw shrubs which grew there not more than forty feet from the path — there being several wild gooseberry bushes there also — and sure enough Poetry was right. I could see a half dozen pear-shaped brown papaws half hidden among the long bright green leaves.

"Let's pick a couple for Circus," Poetry said. Circus, as you know, is the acrobatic member of our gang. He is the only one of us who likes the taste of papaws better than the rest of us.

We swished over to the papaw thicket and in a jiffy I had two of the wrinkled, brown-skinned papaws in my hand. Poetry and I right away each were eating one, it being like a banana inside, only softer, as soft and yellow as the custard Mom puts in her custard pies, and was so sickeningly sweet that only a bite or two was all I could eat. There were always one or two or more large hard seeds in each papaw, which I liked to save and carry around in my pockets, like a boy likes to carry a buckeye, which is supposed to keep him from getting rheumatism, and doesn't, but a boy likes to carry one anyway. I had a buckeye in my pocket right that minute.

All of a sudden Poetry acted like he didn't like the bite of custard-soft yellow papaw flesh he had in his mouth. He turned his face the other way, which you are supposed to do when you have to spit, so other people won't see you do it, and I heard him say, like he had mush in his mouth, "That's the most insipid taste I ever tasted."

"The most *what* kind of taste you ever tasted?" I asked, tasting the same kind of taste myself, and he said, *"Insipid."*

"Just 'cause you know a hundred poems by heart, isn't any reason why you have to use the longest words in the dictionary," I said to him. Picking another wrinkled-skinned softish papaw, I looked down the hill toward the spring, which was still fifty yards away, and saw Circus, himself, halfway up a small sappling that grew there; and down on the ground looking up at him was little red-haired Tom Till, the newest member of our gang, so I said to Poetry, "I'll beat you there." I started to run, with him after me.

Well, in only a few more minutes, we were all there: Big Jim, our leader, who is the only one of us who has any fuzz on his upper lip; Circus, our acrobat; Little Jim, the cutest one of us — in fact the only one of us who *is* cute, most of us trying to be sometimes and not being; Little Tom Till, who has even more freckles and even redder hair than I have; Dragonfly, the spindle-legged and pop-eyed member, who has hay fever and asthma in the summer part of the time; and last of all, myself, red-haired, freckle-faced, fiery-tempered, Bill Collins, Theodore Collins' only boy, whom he sometimes tells people is his "first and worst son" — not meaning it, exactly.

All of us were sitting or lying down in different directions like we generally are at a meeting. When Big Jim got us quiet enough, so he could be heard, he said with a very grim face, "I want everyone of you to vote 'Yes' on the proposition, not because I say so, but because, as soon as you hear about it, you'll know you ought to. It's very important."

"Let's take a 'sight-unseen' vote," Dragonfly said, and I noticed his face had an expression on it like he was getting ready to be allergic to something or other and sneeze. A "sight-unseen" vote was the kind we sometimes took when we all made up our minds that we'd do whatever Big Jim wanted us to without knowing what it was first.

"How many want a 'sight-unseen' vote?" Big Jim asked, and all of us put up our hands except Circus.

Big Jim looked around at all of us, and his eyes stopped at Circus, who had one of my papaws in his hand, and was holding it up looking at it like he was getting ready to take an insipid bite of it.

"What's the matter, Circus?" Big Jim asked. "Why don't you put your hand up?"

"It *is* up," Circus said, "Se-see," he stammered on purpose. "I've got my p-p-papaw up!"

Little Jim giggled, but it didn't seem very funny, especially because I was a little worried by the expression on Big Jim's face, which seemed to say that we were about to vote on something that was not only important, but maybe sad, too.

Well, we took a "sight-unseen" vote and then Big Jim said, "All right, gang, here's what you've just voted 'Yes' to."

While he was starting to tell us, I squirmed myself around into another uncomfortable position behind Poetry's fat back with my red head looking over the top of him. "It's this way," Big Jim's words came out under his fuzzy mustache, "there's a new boy moved into the neighborhood — "

When he got that far, different ones of us, including me, interrupted disgustedly, exclaiming, "NO!" That would mean that there'd probably be another boy for one of us to have to lick before he could belong to our gang. Nearly always when a new boy moved into the Sugar Creek territory, he was the kind of boy that wanted to run the gang, or wanted to introduce a lot of new ideas, or else he was the kind of dumbish person who used swear words which none of the gang used anymore on account of we'd become Christians — and Christians are supposed to have sense enough to have respect for the One who made them. Also, nearly every new boy who had come into our neighborhood used all kinds of filthy talk about girls, and if he was a big boy, Big Jim nearly always got into a fight with him and knocked the living daylights out of him, on account of Big Jim was a special friend of a girl named Sylvia, who was our minister's daughter, and also on account of all our mothers used to be girls, themselves, and it made us all boiling mad to hear filthy words said about them — even though, I'll have to admit, I didn't like girls very well, myself, on account of — well, I just didn't.

So, when Big Jim said, "There's a new boy moved into our neighborhood," it meant our gang would be interrupted for a while.

"Don't worry," Big Jim consoled us, "we won't have to lick him. He's a swell kid. His dad is going to work for my dad this summer, and his mother will help my mother with the canning and things and they'll live in the little brown house Dad and I just finished building. We had to have another hired man this summer, and we just happened to get a family with a boy in it."

"That's better than having one with a *girl* in it," Dragonfly said, he being the only one of us who was more afraid of girls than the rest of us; but Circus gave him a fierce frown — Circus, as you know, having six sisters, and even though sometimes he had small fights with them like brothers sometimes do with their sisters, he still liked them and would fight *for* them at the drop of a hat.

"What's he look like? How big is he?" Little Tom Till wanted to know, and Big Jim said, "He hasn't learned to walk alone yet. You see —"

At that, we all interrupted him with a lot of different exclamations — I, getting a letdown feeling. Imagine calling a special meeting to talk about a baby boy that was so little he couldn't walk yet!

But a jiffy later, Big Jim explained it to us; "He's a spastic. Or, as some people call them, a 'C.P.' He has what is called *cerebral palsy,* and he was born that way. Even though he's ten years old, he can't walk without leaning on something or somebody, and part of the time he wheels himself around in a wheel chair. He can't use his hands very well, and sometimes they won't do what he wants them to do at all; but he can talk pretty well when he's not too excited. He's really a swell kid, and reads a lot and wants to learn to do everything. We'll have to take him with us, sometimes, on our gang trips, and we'll have to act like he is a perfectly normal boy, and not tell him we feel sorry for him, and stuff like that. Dad says so."

Well, when one of our parents says so about something, that nearly always settles it for the whole gang. I was watching Little Jim's face at the time. His cute mouse-like face was always so kind, and I noticed that he had an expression on it that seemed to say he was already sorry for the new boy, and pitied him. "What's his name?" he asked, and when Big Jim said, "Jimmy Lion," it was time for all of us to gasp and exclaim again. Why, that made three *Jims* in our neighborhood! We had Big Jim, our fuzzy mustached leader; Little Jim, our littlest member, and now Jimmy Lion!

"How big is he?" Poetry asked, and when Big Jim said, "Almost halfway between Little Jim and me," Little Tom Till's high-pitched soprano-like voice cut in and said, "Let's call him *Middle-sized* Jim."

We put it to a vote and decided it quicker'n anything.

"Is that all we called this meeting for?" I asked. "If it is, I move we adjourn and let's all go in swimming."

"Second the motion," Poetry said, and "thirded" it by beginning to unbutton his shirt and to roll himself into a sitting position so he could get up quicker.

"Remember," Big Jim said, "we're not to say anything or do anything that will embarrass him, or make him feel he's different from us, 'cause it would have been very easy for any one of us to have been born that way, if — " He stopped, not saying what we all knew he was thinking, on account of boys always do more *thinking* about God than *talking* about Him; but I knew if Big Jim had finished what he had started to say, he would have said, "It would have been easy for any one of us to have been born a spastic, if God, who is the Ruler of everything, had let us be."

Deep down inside of me, I was thankful I had a good strong body that would do everything I wanted it to, although sometimes my parents had a hard time getting my hands and feet to do what *they* wanted them to.

Pretty soon, we were all on our way to the old swimming hole where we'd have the time of our lives. For some reason, though, I felt kind of sad inside on account of the new boy who couldn't walk, so I slowed down and let the gang run on ahead. I was imagining, What if I was a spastic, and couldn't run at all — in fact, couldn't even walk? I looked out toward old Sugar Creek, my very best nature friend, who was making a very happy little rippling sound about twenty feet from me — there being some narrow, fast, sparkling, clear water tumbling over the rocks close to the shore. For a jiffy, I stood there listening to it, looking at the hundreds of sparkles in it, feeling good and sad at the same time.

I didn't know Little Jim had stopped, too, until I heard him sigh behind me.

In case you haven't read any of the other Sugar Creek Gang stories, and don't know how that little guy is always thinking out loud and saying things which my Pop calls philosophical, I'd better tell you that almost any time you can expect that kind of thoughts to come tumbling out of his cherry-shaped mouth.

Anyway, while Little Jim and I were standing side by each, looking at and listening to the happy water with maybe a thousand sparkles in it, he piped up and said, "It's nice to have stars in the daytime, too." Then he, all of a sudden, noticed the rest of the gang laughing and splashing farther up the creek, and away he went, with me chasing right after him.

4

THE FIRST TIME I met Middle-sized Jim, was that very afternoon. I had to go over to his house to take a pie which, by the time we got through swimming and home, Mom had got home first and baked — different ones of the Sugar Creek Gang's mothers having decided to make the Lion family welcome to Sugar Creek by taking them some homemade baked goods. Mom had baked a very nice-smelling raspberry pie, which is my favorite pie, and wrapped it up in oiled paper. I put it in the wire basket on the handle bars of my bicycle, and I, pretty soon, was pedaling like everything toward Big Jim's house, which was across the road from Circus' house, where all of Circus' awkward sisters lived — one of them, named Lucille, who was about my size, not being as awkward as the rest, and would smile back at me across the schoolroom some-times.

When I got past Circus' house, I turned right and went down a narrow county-line road, and pretty soon came to the new brown house Big Jim's Pop made for the Lions to live in.

It was a very pretty little house, I thought. As I put on my brakes and stopped out in front, and leaned my bike up against a maple tree that grew there, I noticed a new tin mailbox with the name, *"John Lion"* on it, which I guessed was Middle-sized Jim's Pop's name. Then I saw Jim, himself, sitting in a wheelchair with some kind of swinging, folding table beside him with a typewriter on it. He was using one of his very awkward-looking hands to sock the different typewriter keys. He hadn't seen me come up or heard me, either, I guess. I didn't know what to say or how to say it, but I remembered our "sight-unseen" vote, so I stood there looking at him as politely as I could. It seemed there wasn't a thing to say to a boy I didn't know, who had cerebral palsy. I noticed he had a pair of braces on his legs, and also, there was a pair of crutches close beside him leaning up against the porch railing.

Well, I took the wrapped-up pie in my hands, feeling how warm it was, and knowing how good it would taste on account of I had helped our family eat maybe five hundred pies like that since I was born a red-haired baby boy. Without knowing I was going to do it, I cleared my throat. Middle-sized Jim heard me, stopped doing what he had awkwardly been doing, and looked me right square in my greenish-grey eyes with a pair just as greenish-grey as mine, and said, with his neck jerking a little and leaning toward the left, "I'm sorry; I didn't see you." He raised his kind of friendly voice and called, "Mother! We have company!" Then his eyes looked out toward the tree where my bike was and he said, "I'm going to learn to ride a bike sometime. I've earned almost enough money to buy one."

Just like that, I thought. It was easy to get acquainted with him. He didn't act bashful or embarrassed, but I thought, "How in the world can he learn to ride a bicycle?"

"I have to learn to walk first," he said.

Well, we talked a little while about different things and pretty soon I was on my way home with the last thing he had said tumbling around in my mind, which was, "Anytime you need any letters typed, bring them over, and I'll type them for you free. I have a big library of books, too — books on nature especially — flowers and trees and birds and all kinds of animals and reptiles such as snakes and turtles — anything you want to know about."

I decided if Pop didn't know what kind of snake I'd killed that afternoon, maybe Middle-sized Jim could look it up for me in one of his nature books.

When I came pedaling up to "Theodore Collins" on our mailbox, I could see my reddish-brown-mustached, bushy-eybrowed Pop in our garden by the twin pignut trees. He had a hoe in his hands and was hoeing like a house afire. I wanted, the worst way, to swing happily into the drive, lean my bike up against the side of our tool shed, which is beside the grape arbor, and yell out to Pop about the big snake I'd killed, and then go dashing over to him and show it to him, lying there in the weeds beside the rail fence; but for some reason, I was thinking about the dictionary definition of *several* which was, "more than one or two, but not many."

Knowing that Pop had probably hoed several rows of potatoes, himself, and *his* several would not only be more than one or two, but maybe five or six, I decided to go out to the barn and start to gather the eggs. That is, I decided it, then right away, I *un*-decided it. When Pop called to me in a gruff voice, saying, "WILLIAM!" I knew there was something I had done wrong or that I hadn't done right, or just hadn't done and should have, because that is the only time he ever calls me *William*.

"What?" I yelled back as cheerfully as I could. "I'm going to gather the eggs!"

"Come here!" Pop's voice sounded like he meant business so I denied myself the privilege of gathering the eggs. Not wanting him to think I was worried about the several rows of potatoes that were left unhoed, I started to whistle, and also to sing a little — in fact, the tune was the one about, "One little word shall fell him."

"Hurry up!" Pop called, and I hurried a little. Pop leaned on his hoe till I got to the garden fence, then he said, "You like our new dictionary, Bill?"

I felt myself blushing all the way up to the roots of my red hair. Had Pop guessed what word I had looked up, and was he going to give me a scolding of some kind?

"You left the dictionary open," he said. "You should never leave a good book open on a windy, dusty afternoon like it was today." Then just like he wanted to change the subject, Pop said, "What else did you do today?"

I breathed a sigh of wonderful relief and said cheerfully, "I killed a great big ugly heavy-bodied snake. I don't know what kind it is. I never saw such a fierce snake in my life. He's lying dead there in the weeds right behind you."

In a jiffy, I was in the garden with Pop, and he and I were looking around in the weeds below the place where Poetry had draped the snake over the fence, but say! That great big fierce-looking dead snake wasn't there anywhere!

"That's funny," I said, puzzled.

"What did he look like?" Pop asked me, holding his hoe in both hands like he was ready to cut a snake in two if he saw one that was alive.

When I told him it was reddish-yellow with brown blotches on it and that it puffed out its neck fiercely and struck at me and hissed and that its nose was turned up like a scoop shovel, Pop's bushy eyebrows went down, and he looked serious. "Where did you say he was when you first saw him?"

"Lying in the path halfway between here and the stile — all by himself."

"And were you all by *yourself,* without a thing with which to protect yourself?" Pop's voice was anxious.

"Except for a clod of dirt as big around as Charlotte Ann's head, which I missed him with when I threw it at him. But I threw my *voice* at him, too, and that killed him, scared to death," I said. "The very minute the clod struck close to his three-inch-wide head and puffed-out neck, he twisted himself up into several knots, plopped over on his back, and died. Poetry came along just then, and we poked at him with a stick to see if he was really dead, and he was. Poetry picked him up by the tail, then, and draped him over the fence right here."

"Sounds like a fish story," Pop said. "You're sure you're not kidding me?"

"It's the truth," I said, still looking for the greenish-yellow-stomached snake.

"You say he puffed out his neck and head and hissed at you?"

"Yes, sir."

Pop's face looked like he believed me, then he said, "Sounds like a *hissing adder* or a *puff adder*. If it was, you're lucky to be alive, Bill Collins."

At that, Pop looked around very carefully to see if he could still find it, but he couldn't. We did find Warty, though, who had been hiding in the shade of a very large plantain leaf. When Pop saw him, he said, "Well, hello, Warty! Glad to see *you're* still alive, anyway," I noticed he called both Warty and me by the names he liked us by, and I felt better, but was still kind of tense inside. Where, I thought, was the hissing adder now?

Just that second, there was the sound of chickens making about a hundred scared squawks in our chicken yard. I looked up in time to see a big chicken hawk swooping down from the top of one of the twin pignut trees. He made a dive through the sky straight for a little lonely, fluffy, peeping chicken by the grape arbor, and the next thing I knew, the hawk was up in the air again, and the soft, fluffy little baby chick was gone.

"That's what happened to your snake," Pop said. "Chicken hawks like snakes, too."

And maybe Pop was right. In fact I knew he was, until the next day when I was finishing hoeing several more rows of potatoes. This time my *several* was not only more than one or two, but it seemed like it was more than *many*.

Poetry was there, too. He had stopped at the Lions' den, as Middle-sized Jim called their house, and wheeled him over in his wheel chair, and Middle-sized Jim had showed us how he could almost walk without his crutches; but every time after he had taken a few steps he fell ker-sprawlety-plop. While we were helping him up he'd say, "It didn't hurt a bit. I'm used to it," and he would be grinning like he was having fun.

We told him the snake story. "A great big chicken hawk ate him up," I said.

But Middle-sized Jim spoiled our story for

us by saying, "Chicken hawks won't eat dead things unless they kill them, themselves."

I looked up from my hoeing, and I thought he had a mischievous grin on his face, although I couldn't tell for sure on account of he was smiling almost all the time anyway.

Well, after what seemed like a terribly long time, I finished hoeing the last row, and since we were all thirsty we decided to go down to the stile to get a drink at the iron pitcher pump there, rather than at the pump at the end of the board walk near our house.

Middle-sized Jim could make it O.K. with his crutches, and several times he took a couple steps by himself before losing his balance and falling, and landing all tangled up in the dust of the path; but he'd just laugh, and we'd help him up and go on. And then, all of a sudden, he let out a yell. "Look! *There's* your dead snake taking a sun bath!"

I looked, and what to my wondering eyes should appear, but a great big reddish-yellow snake as big as the one I had killed yesterday.

5

A BOY HAS A HARD TIME believing his eyes when the mind under his red hair tells him that what he sees isn't so. Yesterday, we'd picked up a dead snake and carried him to the rail fence that enclosed our garden and had draped him over the top rail and left him, and a chicken hawk had eaten him, but to-day — twenty-four hours later — here he was, the same great big heavy-bodied savage-looking snake, lying alive out in the middle of the field!

Say, we were already close to him; and just like he'd done yesterday, he acted as mad as anything. He was puffing out his neck and head and hissing and striking in our direction like he wanted to kill us quick, and would if we came any closer.

"He's mad 'cause we woke him up out of his sleep," Poetry said.

"We interrupted his bath, and he probably wanted privacy," Middle-sized Jim said.

I had a big stick with me this time and I was going to be sure we really killed him. I started to make a rush at the snake and take a swipe at his upraised head, but Middle-sized Jim's excited voice stopped me, saying, "Don't, Bill! Wait! I've got an idea! That's probably a brother or a wife of the one you killed yesterday! Let's see if you can scare *this* one to death!"

I looked at his grinning face, but couldn't tell whether he was making fun of me or not. He was having a little trouble balancing himself with his crutches, so I made a dive in his direction to keep from falling just as Poetry said, "Let's see what *my* voice will do."

Without waiting for us to let him, Poetry picked up a big clod like the one I'd had yesterday, and squashed it into a thousand pieces of dirt and dust about a foot from the snake's hissing head, and yelled down at it fiercely, making up a poem at the same time saying:

"You great big ugly squirming lummox,
Get over on your back and turn up your
    stomach!"

Well, you can believe it or not, but just like the snake I'd done that to yesterday, that reddish-yellow, brown-splotched snake, all of a sudden went into contortions like a boy having a spasm from eating too many green apples or green grapes or something, and the next thing we knew, there he was, over on his back with his pretty greenish-yellow stomach shining in the sun, and he wasn't even moving a muscle! *Imagine* that!

That tickled Middle-sized Jim. "I knew it. I *knew* it!" he exclaimed. "It's a *hog-nosed* snake! That's the way they do when they're cornered. First, they act very fierce like they are the most dangerous snake in the world, and try to scare you away, but if you don't go and they think their lives are in danger, they'll play dead like a 'possum in the woods, and plop over like that and stay that way. I have a book in my library that tells about it."

It made sense, but not quite enough to suit me, so I said, "Yes, but we poked at it, and carried it by the tail and draped it over the rail fence and everything!"

"That's what the book says, but when you go away and leave a hog-nosed snake, it looks around to see if you are really gone, and see-ing a chance to escape, it quickly crawls away.

"It doesn't stay dead," Middle-sized Jim ex-plained, and even as he said it, and I was mad at myself for being fooled yesterday, I couldn't help but remember a sermon which Sylvia's Pop had preached once in the Sugar Creek Church when he had said that Satan who in the Bible is called, "That Old Serpent," had been licked at the Cross when Jesus had died for our sins, but that Satan wouldn't give up. He still acted like he owned the world, and if anybody would let him, he would be his boss.

Poetry interrupted my thoughts by saying, "Let's *really* kill him." He started to do what I had started to do, but Middle-sized Jim stopped him just like he had me and said, "No, let's have some fun! Pick him up by the tail and lay him down on his *stomach* again and see what happens."

"Pop says it's a *puff adder*, and they're ter-ribly dangerous," I said.

"That's just another name for the *hog-nosed* snake," Middle-sized Jim said. "They act more dangerous than even a copperhead, but they're harmless. Go ahead, turn him over!"

I turned him over with my stick and — would you believe it? — the funniest thing happened. That heavy-bodied, reddish-brown and yellow snake was no sooner on his stomach than he twisted himself into and out of a half knot and plopped himself over on his back again, and was as quiet as a dead mouse; and then we knew that he'd actually been playing dead, and that this was probably the same one I thought I'd killed yesterday. He looked silly lying there now, and I could almost imagine that he had a grin on the long slit-shaped mouth on his hog-nosed head.

"Now, let's go off and leave him awhile. Let's see how long he will wait before he quits playing 'possum and crawls away," Middle-sized Jim said.

It seemed like a chance to have some more fun, so we left the snake and went down the path toward the stile to get the drink of water we had started out to get in the first place.

Say, we got clear to the pump, Poetry and I walking backwards part of the time, and looking back most of the time, to see how soon our dead snake would become a live one. Poetry was beginning to pump the pump while I held one of the paper cups, which Pop kept there in a rain-proof container — Pop not leaving any other kind of cup there on account of he wanted to teach boys and other people not to all drink out of the same cup on account of it might spread different kinds of diseases.

All of an excited sudden, Middle-sized Jim let out a yell and said, "Look! There he goes! See him? He's heading back to the garden!"

Poetry stopped pumping. I dropped my cup of water and grabbed up my stick. This time there was going to be a dead snake for sure. As fast as I could, with Poetry at my heels, I dashed back across the bare field. Say, I never saw a snake run so fast in my life — glide, rather, which is the way snakes move. Boy, he was really going!

"Hurry up!" I yelled over my shoulder at Poetry, and he came puffing after me at a very noisy, dusty rate. I hoped I could make it before the snake got to the pignut trees and lost himself in the weeds by the rail fence where we couldn't find him.

And then the queerest thing happened. It was so interesting and exciting and also so astonishing that it almost made me forget the snake. Right that second from behind me, I heard Middle-sized Jim's voice yelling, "Hey you guys! Don't kill him! Let him live!"

I looked back over my shoulder, and there was our new spastic friend, who hadn't walked five feet in his life without holding on to someone or something, and he was running after us, dragging his crutches! *Running!* A boy who couldn't even walk, was *running!* It didn't make sense. He wasn't running straight like the members of our gang did, but he was running almost as fast as Poetry and I.

I took my eyes off the snake for half a jiffy, and so also did Poetry, and I yelled back to Middle-sized Jim. "Hey," I said, "you're *running!*"

But I wished I hadn't said it, for the minute Middle-sized Jim heard me, he got a queer expression on his face like he had just lost something that was worth a million dollars, and the next thing I knew, he was struggling to keep his balance. A second later, down he went, ker-sprawlety-plop onto the ground, stirring up a cloud of dust which the wind picked up and blew across the field toward the stile, like powdered snow blowing across the field in the wintertime.

*   *   *

Well, that was the first time Middle-sized Jim ever really walked, and he had not only walked, but he had run. He was so tickled, he could hardly believe it himself. We were so excited about it that we let our snake get away, and we never saw him again until two weeks later when he turned up in the most interesting way you could ever imagine.

First, though, I'd better explain that Middle-sized Jim's doctor said that he had learned to walk, or rather run, because he had got what is called, "absolute concentration" or something, and he got it when he saw the snake running away, and Poetry and me trying to catch it; he had wanted to stop us from killing it because he knew it wasn't a dangerous snake. He had forgotten all about his not being able to run. Seeing us do it, he had been so excited, that he ran, himself. His running wasn't like any ordinary boy's though. It was half-run and half-lurch, but he could do it without his crutches, which was wonderful.

That was the beginning of a much happier life for Middle-sized Jim. Also it happened to be the very thing which makes this story the most exciting one we'd had in a long time, which, pretty soon, I'll tell you about.

Before I do, I have to tell you where we found old Hog-nose again, and what he was doing and why. I also have to tell you a little more about Warty, my Pop's favorite toad friend and his own very exciting adventure.

I guess I didn't realize that hog-nosed snakes and garter snakes would rather eat a toad for supper than a boy would rather eat a plateful of raw-fried potatoes and bread and butter when he is hungry. But, they would; only I, as I said, didn't realize it, and, of course, I didn't know that that snake had been hanging around our garden on purpose because he had his appetite set on making a delicious supper out of Warty.

Warty must have guessed that old Hog-nose was laying for him, because one day he disappeared, and we didn't see him around the

garden for maybe a week; and there were all
kinds of cutworms that kept snipping off
Mom's baby beans and sugar corn shoots, and
there didn't seem to be much we could do to
stop them.

"Maybe Warty finds all the cutworms he
can stuff himself with, out in the corn field,"
Mom said one day, and maybe she was right.
Anyway, several days later — one or two, but
not many — I was coming home from having
been fishing down in the branch with Dragonfly, and on the way back, I was halfway
through one of our other potato patches,
which is quite a ways from our regular garden,
when I was startled by a clumsy movement at
my feet. Looking down, I saw a large lazy-
looking brown toad in the skimpy shade of a
wild carrot weed, which somebody's boy
should have pulled long ago — the wild carrot or Queen Anne's lace, which is one of its
other names, being Pop's worst hated weed.
Mom liked to look at its pretty lace-like flowers
which, when they are only half opened, are all in
a little circle with a hollow in the middle, which
is the reason why it is sometimes called by

still another name, Bird's Nest. But Pop always made me pull up all the Queen Anne's lace I could find on account of he says it is a very bad weed with very stubborn roots, and if you leave one for a year, next year there'll be a great big family of them to get rid of.

As soon as I saw Pop's toad friend, I said down to him cheerfully, "Why, hello, Warty, old pal! Am I glad to see you! Will Mom ever be tickled!"

I decided to run and tell Mom about it right away. I started to start to the house. Then I changed my mind because an interesting plan popped into my head. In a jiffy, I had Warty picked up in a big handkerchief I had in my pocket, not exactly wanting to handle him with my bare hands because right under a toad's warty skin there are glands which give off a bitter fluid of some kind that is just a little bit poisonous. If a dumb puppy dog tries to pick up a toad to play with it, he quick drops it, not liking the toad's taste. I was afraid Warty wouldn't know I was a friend, and I'd maybe get some poisonous gland fluid on my bare hands. Some boys think toads

cause warts on a boy's hands, but they don't.
It makes Pop mad to hear anybody say that
about an innocent toad 'cause it isn't so at all.

Anyway, I wrapped up Warty in my handkerchief, leaving his nose out so he could
breathe. Holding him tight so he wouldn't
squirm himself out of my grasp, I carried him
back to the garden where Mom's cabbage
plants needed him to take care of them.

To be sure Warty wouldn't hop away again,
I tied the end of my fishing line around the
joint of one of his fat legs, leaving the rest of
the long line on the reel on my fishing pole, so
Warty would be free to hop all over the garden and gobble up all the cutworms he could
find that night — for as you maybe know cutworms always do their cutting off of cabbage
plants and young corn shoots at night.

"There you are, my friend," I said to Warty, as soon as I had him tied to the end of the
line. "Now see to it that you behave yourself
and stay here where we need you a lot worse
than we do down yonder in that other potato
patch."

Mom certainly was tickled when I told her
Warty was back again — and that I'd brought

him myself. I didn't tell her about tying him up.

It was sort of like tethering out our old one-eared cow on a long rope where she can eat grass in every direction for quite a long ways, but she can't get away to eat where she is not supposed to.

At the supper table that night, Pop and Mom and Charlotte Ann and I sat very quiet for a minute like we always do before we eat, with our heads bowed while Pop asked the blessing. For a short jiffy I opened my eyes and looked at Mom's kind of grayish-brown hair all combed nice and pretty like she hurries up and combs it whenever she knows Pop is coming home from working in the field. I also noticed Pop's reddish-brown hair and his long shaggy, reddish-brown eyebrows, which he also combs sometimes, and won't let the barber clip them shorter like barbers try to do, Pop says, if you don't stop them; and also I saw our brown-haired baby sister's head. I noticed she had her hands unfolded, and her eyes wide open, and she was looking around at different things. Without knowing I was going to do it, I whispered to her, saying, "Sh! Charlotte Ann! Shut your eyes! Pop is going to ask the blessing! You're supposed to have your eyes shut!"

Pop probably heard me, but didn't pay any attention to me. In his prayer, he said that we were thankful for the food before us, which I certainly was 'cause it was raw-fried potatoes, bread and butter, apple pie and cheese, some cold chicken which was left over from dinner. There was also a bottle of cod-liver oil from which Mom was going to put half a spoonful into Charlotte Ann's orange juice as soon as Pop finished praying. In fact, right that second, Charlotte Ann was stretching one hand as far as she could toward the glass of orange juice — like maybe Warty, right that very minute, was straining at the end of my fishing line for a nice juicy cutworm.

Pop's prayer was kind of short, like it sometimes is at supper time when he knows all of us are hungry and tired, but I remember he prayed for Middle-sized Jim, saying, "Dear Father, we pray that Thou wilt bless all the fine boys and girls in the world who were born like Jimmy Lion; help people to understand them and to love them. We thank Thee for

the blessing Jimmy has been to all of us, with
his sunny disposition and his eager mind.
Help us all to apply ourselves to our studies
as earnestly as he does . . . "

When Pop got that far, I felt maybe he was
praying for me, too, and I couldn't tell for
sure whether he was talking to God or to me,
but it seemed like maybe I ought to study a
little harder that fall when school started.

Mom, hearing Pop pray for Jimmy, must
have been reminded of the hog-nosed snake
that had disappeared a week or two ago; and
that must have reminded her of my hands,
'cause the very second Pop finished his prayer,
she looked straight at my hands, which were
already busy spreading butter on a slice of
her homemade bread. I quick spoke up and
said — just to show her I knew what she was
thinking about — "I didn't touch Warty at
all. I used my handkerchief." Then I saw
Mom's face get a strange expression on it, and
I knew I'd made a mistake even before she
said, "You mean you used one of your nice
white handkerchiefs to pick up a dirty toad!"

I had to think of something to defend myself with, quick, so I said, "It wasn't *all* white,

it already had blood stains on it from trying
to —"

"Blood!" Mom said, astonished.

"I — yes, ma'am," I said, unusually polite.
"Dragonfly and I were wading in the branch,
and he stepped on a sharp stone and cut his
foot and I had to help him stop it from bleed-
ing."

"You were wading in the *branch?*" Pop
said with an exclamation point in his voice.
He looked around the edge of the table at my
overalls to see if, when I'd had them rolled up
and was in the water, the trouser legs had
come down like they sometimes do and had
gotten wet.

"We didn't have our overalls *on,*" I said.
"It was too deep there."

"*What?*" Pop asked. "The only place the
branch is deep is down near where it empties
into the creek and that's close to the *road*. I
hope you boys didn't wade out there with
your clothes off, *that* close to the road."

"We had to," I said. "We were looking for
something we had lost."

"You lost something? . . . *Bill Collins!*"

Mom said. "You haven't lost anything important, I hope!"

"Just a piece of fishing line that got fastened onto the bottom on a snag."

"Did you have to break your new line?" Pop asked. And I said, yawning, like it didn't matter much, "Oh, a few feet, maybe."

"Several?" Pop asked, and out of the corner of my eye, as I poked into my mouth a forkful of swell-tasting, raw-fried potatoes, I saw that he had a twinkle in his eyes, and I knew he wasn't mad at me at all for having hoed only three rows of potatoes that other afternoon.

"I'll try to make it six or seven next time," I said to Pop, and Mom said, "You mean you'll try to lose more line next time?"

Pop looked at me and winked, and I made up my mind that the very next time I had to hoe several rows of potatoes, I'd see if I could stretch the word "several" until it was almost as long as "many."

When I was in my room that night with the light out, and was getting ready to drop into bed on the nice clean sheets Mom had put on that very day, I looked out the window to the moonlit garden where Warty was tethered. I was a little worried about him, wondering if he would get himself tangled up in the line before he even got started on his trips up and down the sweet-corn rows for cutworms.

Warty really knows how to gobble them up, too, just like he does a fly or a mosquito or a grub or anything else in the insect family that gets within two inches of his mouth. Warty's tongue isn't fastened at the *back* of his mouth like mine is, but at the *front,* and he can, all of a terribly fast sudden, flip his tongue out like it was a whip with a lash on the end. If there is a fly buzzing around his head, quicker than nothing there isn't any fly, and the only way you know Warty got him is when you see the tiny movement he makes in his throat when he swallows. Once Pop and I watched Warty hopping down one of Mom's bean rows, and even though we didn't see his long sticky whip-like tongue catch a single bug, when he got to the end of the row, there wasn't a one left.

As I said, I was looking out the window toward our moonlit garden. I cocked one ear in Warty's direction to see if I could hear my reel clicking, like it does when I'm fishing and get a bite. But as hard as I listened, I couldn't hear a thing except the leaves of the ivy vine that grew across the upper part of the window, rustling in the wind.

So I quick dropped down on my knees to pray a sort of tired prayer to the heavenly Father Whom my parents had begun to teach me to pray to when I was as little as Charlotte Ann, and I've been doing it ever since. I was so tired I couldn't think straight. Maybe my words were mixed up a little, but it seemed like even though God might be pretty busy running such a big world and a whole sky full of stars and planets and things, still I just sort of knew that He liked boys and was interested in the things they like to do. It also seemed like He even liked me, Bill Collins, and that He wasn't holding it against me for praying such an ordinary prayer. I guess I must have gotten Pop's supper-time prayer mixed up in mine, although I wasn't sure, but

I sort of heard myself saying, "Bless Middle-sized Jim and take care of him . . . He's been a blessing to all of us."

I don't remember finishing my prayer at all, but when I woke up sometime in the middle of the night, I was in bed, so I must have climbed in. I had been dreaming that I was fishing and had hooked a terribly big fish like the kind the gang sometimes catches on our northern fishing trips. In my dream, the reel was singing and singing and the line was running out clear to the end, and I was trying to hold onto the pole, and not lose my fish. That was when I woke up. Say, I was sure I had heard a noise out in the garden.

I lay quiet for a second, my heart pounding. I rolled over to sit on the edge of the bed, leaned forward to the open window, and then I *knew* I was hearing something. I was hearing my reel make little sharp jerking sounds like the line was being unwound only a little at a time.

Then I grinned to myself there in the moonlight, as in my mind's eye, I saw Warty hopping down a row of Mom's young cabbage plants with his lightning-quick, sticky tongue flipping in and out, gobbling up cutworms, and other plant enemies.

I sighed happily, and went back to sleep until morning. Then, just like I do when there is something very interesting to get up for, I sprang out of bed, shoved myself into my clothes, and, two steps at a time, was on my way downstairs to see how much of my fishing line had been unwound, and if Warty had worked himself loose and run away again.

6

I FORGOT that I was up even earlier than
Mom, herself, and even Pop, *himself*. Certainly, I was up before Charlotte Ann was supposed to be. So, when I heard the screen door
slam behind me, as I dashed out past our
iron pitcher pump, I realized that the loud
noise the door had made, would probably
wake up Charlotte Ann; and once she waked
up in the morning, that was the end of it for
any sleep any of the rest of the family wanted
to get.

But it was too late now to go back to shut
the door "like a gentleman," as my parents
tell me is the way to do it, so I dashed on till
I came to within about ten feet of the rail
fence. Not knowing what to expect, I crept
forward quietly, till I got to where I could see
my fishing pole. The first thing I noticed was
that the reel was nearly all unwound, so I
figured Warty must have done quite a lot of

traveling. I peeked through the fence, let my eyes run down the length of the line, which had threaded its way around through the potatoes and corn and beans and cabbage plants. Away over at the other side of the garden, not far from the pignut trees, it disappeared in the tall weeds.

What would Warty be doing out there in the weeds? I wondered. It wasn't hot enough for him to be looking for shade because even the sun wasn't up yet, it was so early. Climbing over the fence, I followed the trail of the line until I came to where it disappeared. I wondered if Warty had got tangled up in the weeds or what. And then, all of a sudden, in a little open space in the weeds, I saw something that made me stop stock still and stare. It was one of the saddest and most exciting sights I ever saw in my life. I saw a great big hog-nosed snake fastened onto my line instead of Warty. In fact, the line was right in his mouth! What on earth! I thought.

And then, all of a sickening sudden, I knew what had happened. I knew it because I had seen a pair of toad's legs sticking out of the snake's mouth. The legs were kicking and making the snake look like he had two great big live horns on his head. That fierce-looking hog-nosed snake had swallowed my friend, Warty, headfirst all the way down to his legs!

I must have gotten there more quietly than I thought, 'cause the snake didn't even seem to realize I was watching him. He kept struggling and struggling with Warty, his head and neck puffed out much farther than they had been the day I'd first seen him and he had been hissing at me.

Warty still hadn't given up, or those two legs wouldn't have been kicking and squirming, and I knew he was trying to back out. The snake's mouth kept working and working, and it seemed like he was trying to pull Warty in, as if his body was a gunny sack, and he was working the end of the sack up around Warty's fat sides.

I was so surprised, and also so horrified at what I knew was happening — and realizing that maybe I was to blame for tieing Warty up, so he couldn't get away — that I was like I was paralyzed. I couldn't even scream for Pop to come to see if he could still save Warty.

And then, the next thing I knew, there was a sort of walking movement in the snake's neck, and Warty's two legs disappeared; and down below the snake's head, I saw a big bulge which meant that our friendly garden toad was completely swallowed.

Well, I knew there wasn't any use getting hold of my fishing line, and trying to pull Warty out because Middle-sized Jim had told me that snakes' teeth are slanted back into their mouths and throats, and I could never pull Warty out.

And then, I got the idea. If Warty wasn't dead yet, and if his tough toad skin had only been scratched or pricked by the snake's sharp teeth, he might still be alive, and that idea brought me to quick life. If you have read some of the other Sugar Creek Gang stories, you know that I had already made up my mind I was going to be a doctor some day, and give people medicine to make them well. I would also operate on people. As quick as I got the idea, I raced across the garden, vaulted over the fence and made a wild dive to the toolhouse where we kept our hoes and spades. I was going to quick grab up a hoe, race madly back to the garden, which Warty out of his kind heart had been looking after for us. I was going to get to Warty before old Hognose had a chance to start digesting him, slice the snake in two right close to the place where Warty was, and see if I could get Warty out, still alive. I would use the hoe to chop the snake in two, and my boy scout knife to do any other operating on him I had to, to get Warty out.

Just as I came out of the tool shed with the hoe, Pop came out of our house's back door, saw me and exclaimed with irony in his voice, "Well, what do you know!" He must have been astonished. He also must have felt mischievous 'cause he said to me, "Well, of all things! Bill Collins has gotten ambitious!" — which is a word to describe people who think of doing things without being told to, and who, also, maybe like to work.

But I couldn't be bothered with anything funny. "Quick!" I yelled to Pop, "Follow me, and help me save Warty's life! He's gotten himself swallowed by a snake!"

A lot of our chickens must have thought that so much noisy excitement close to our house meant something for them to eat 'cause a whole flock of maybe forty hens came rushing toward us, half running and half flying, like they sometimes do when Mom comes out the kitchen door with a panful of something she's going to toss out to them. Anyway, when I quick dived back to the garden yelling for Pop to follow me, I stumbled over a couple of excited hens, one of them being Old Bent Comb who lays her eggs in our haymow. Those two old hens and the rest of the chickens went scattering in every main direction there is, and also, in all the other little directions there are in between, making a noisy scared path for me to run through on my way back to Warty.

"Hurry up!" I yelled back to Pop over my shoulder. At the garden, I vaulted over the fence, swished through the dusty garden as quick as I could without stepping on any sugar corn or cabbages.

Say, when I got there, I found out that Pop had not only come to quick life and followed me, but he had also used his head and had stopped at Mom's clothesline and brought with him a forked stick which we used as a clothesline prop; and in almost less time than I can write it for you, Pop and I went into action.

Maybe I'd better tell you though that one time the year before, Pop and our doctor had let me watch a boy having his appendix cut out. So even while I was scared and excited and worried about Warty, I imagined myself to be a doctor, and I gave quick sharp orders to Pop, like a doctor giving them to his nurse, while I held onto my fishing line so old Hognose couldn't get away. "Quick! Get that forked clothesline prop down on his neck! Pin him to the ground! there — just above the bulge Warty makes!"

And Pop did.

But say! That snake's head being pinned to the ground made the tail and the rest of his ugly heavy body come to the most excited life you ever saw. It seemed like he was trying to twist himself into and. out of a million twists and wiggles and knots. I don't know how I ever did what I did, but I did, and I certainly wasn't smart enough to think that fast either, but in a jiffy I was standing on the body of the snake with my right foot and was ready to begin my first surgical operation.

"Hey," Pop said suddenly, trying to be mischievous at a very serious time, "you can't perform an operation without first giving the patient an anesthetic," — which any boy knows is a medicine a doctor uses on a patient before he operates, so as to kill the pain.

I didn't pay any more attention to Pop's half-funny remark than anything. I had my official boy scout knife out of my pocket, and was opening its sharp cutting blade.

"Aren't you going to kill the pain first?" Pop asked, still with a mischievous grin in his voice.

"I'm going to kill the *snake*," I said. With my left hand, I grabbed the snake's heavy body halfway between my foot and Warty's bulge and started to operate just as Pop said, "All good doctors wash their hands with soap before they perform an operation."

I couldn't be bothered. All I could think of was my friend Warty inside that bulge where he couldn't get a breath of fresh air, so

I said, "This good doctor will wash his hands *after* the operation."

"Your mother will see to that," Pop remarked.

I was down on my left knee in the garden dirt, my right foot still on the snake's body.

"Never mind making a fancy incision," Pop said. "Just cut him in two and let Warty hop out by himself."

Well, the rest of the operation isn't very pleasant to write about, so I won't write about it. Besides, it was too sad.

"Poor Warty," Pop said, after it was all over and Warty lay motionless on the ground. It looked like he was completely dead. I looked down at him and felt my eyes stinging, and I knew if I had been a little littler, I'd maybe have cried.

"It's all my fault," I said, feeling very sad. "If I hadn't tied him up, he could have gotten away."

"Maybe not," Pop said. "Snakes like that live on toads and frogs — toads especially — and they know how to catch them without help."

I cut my line off, and Pop dug a hole in the corner of the garden for Warty's grave, and there we buried him.

We dug another grave for the snake, and covered them both up.

Pop and I were getting to be better and better friends, I thought, as we carried the hoe back toward the tool shed. He was not only my great big Daddy, who was my Mom's husband, but he was a pretty nice person also, even if he was a father.

Just then Mom opened the back door of our house and stood in the doorway and looked at us with a question mark in her eyes. *"Now* what have you two boys been up to?" she asked.

"Bill just performed a surgical operation," Pop said, and added, "and the patient died."

"We just had a *funeral,"* I said to Mom.

"A funeral?"

"Warty," I said.

We told Mom everything and her eyes took on a faraway expression. I thought I saw tears in them, but she changed the subject by saying, "If the doctor and the undertaker will

get washed up, we'll have breakfast in just a
few jiffies," which we did.

Well, that was the end of this part of the
story, the end also of both the toad and the
snake. It was too terribly bad that Warty had
to die, I thought, but it was a good thing there
had been a big hog-nosed snake around our
garden on account of it was when Middle-
sized Jim got excited that day when the snake
had been trying to glide away, that Middle-
sized Jim had got what his doctor called "absolute concentration," and had learned to
walk and even to run. From then on, he could
do both, although, as I said, his run was more
of a lurch than a run.

Also, it was Middle-sized Jim's learning to
walk and run that made the most important
part of this story happen. I'll get going on that
just as soon as I can. First, though, I have to
tell you about what happened in our garden
the next day when Little Jim came over to our
house. He had come to get a copy of one of
Mom's recipes for making a very special kind
of pie which Little Jim's Mom had tasted at
a potluck dinner at their Sunday school class
party. I think it was called a lemon meringue

or something. Mom had surprised all the other Sugar Creek mothers by mixing in some chopped black walnut kernels, and it had tasted wonderful.

Little Jim had wanted to know the whole story about Warty, just like it happened to me and Pop. Poetry was already at my home and he and I were just finishing making a couple of twig whistles and were blowing them, making a lot of boy noise. We took Little Jim out to the garden, and I told the whole story over again, having already told it to Poetry. Little Jim always listened to stories with his face as well as with both ears, his small mouse-like face with its cherry-shaped mouth getting a lot of different kinds of expressions on it while he listened.

When I finished, we were all standing near Warty's grave where Poetry had erected a shingle with a poem on it, which he had written himself, and which was:

"Here lies Warty, the farmer's best friend —
How sad that he had such a terrible end!"

I thought I noticed tears in Little Jim's eyes as he stood looking down at Poetry's poetry. Then, like he often does when he has a couple of tears which he doesn't want anybody to see, he turned his face away, gave his head a quick toss, and when he looked back again, the tears had disappeared. They had fallen on one of Mom's cabbage plants, maybe. If a cabbage plant could think, it'd probably have been surprised, wondering if it had started to rain salt water instead of rain water.

"Where'd you bury the *snake?*" Little Jim asked.

"Right over there," I said, pointing to a little mound of clay without any marker.

Little Jim walked over to it. Then all of a sudden, he let out a gasp and said, "Hey, you guys! Come here! Look!"

Well, you could have knocked me over with the seedpod of a milkweed when I saw what I saw, which was about nine inches from Little Jim's brown bare dusty feet. It was a great big blinking, brown-skinned, warty-looking toad!

Poetry saw it at the same time, and exclaimed, "IT'S WARTY! HE'S COME BACK TO LIFE!"

I looked down at the warty-skinned amphibian, which is what Middle-sized Jim says a toad is, and he actually did look exactly like Warty. He was blinking his glassy eyes like he was thinking some kind of lazy, mischievous thoughts; but it just couldn't be Warty, I thought, and said so. "He doesn't have any snake teeth marks on him."

"Maybe they healed up," Little Jim said.

"They couldn't in only one day," Poetry said.

"The only way to know for sure, is to dig into his grave to see if he came to life and crawled out," I said.

Pop, hearing all the excitement, came out of the barn. I saw him and yelled to him, "Hey Pop! Come here!"

In a few jiffies, Pop was there with us, and we were all standing in a little half circle looking down at the toad's simpish, blinking eyes. Pop reached out the toe of his heavy shoe, and touched the toad which filled himself up with air, like toads do, and looked as tight as a toy balloon at a county fair.

"Do you suppose, maybe, this one is Warty, instead of the one that got swallowed yesterday?" I asked Pop.

Poetry, feeling extra mischievous that day, made up a new poem real quick, and said,

"His tummy is so round and firm
Because he ate a fat cutworm."

Pop ignored Poetry's poetry, stooped down and said in a kind, friendly voice, "Warty, my friend, let's have a look at your left front foot to see if you are you, or if that's you over there under that tombstone," meaning under Poetry's shingle.

Say, when Pop leaned down to Warty, and, with a small stick, tried to get his front foot out where we could see it, all of a clumsy sudden that big fat toad gave an acrobatic flip, and landed on his back with his brownish stomach exposed to the sky.

"What on *earth!*" I said, remembering the hog-nosed snake had done the same thing himself.

Pop ignored my exclamation and said, "Yep, that's Warty! Look! See, there's one toe missing on his left front foot. I accidentally cut it off a week or two ago when I was hoeing several rows of potatoes, and the very next day, he disappeared, and I thought that was why he had run away. I thought he didn't like me anymore, and wasn't going to oblige the Collins family any longer by eating up our cutworms. I didn't know, of course, that the real reason he ran away, was because he was afraid of the snake . . . Well, well, well, Warty, I won't hurt you. You can get right back on your tummy again."

None of us said anything for a jiffy, as Pop made us all step back about ten or fifteen feet. "Now keep your eyes on him," Pop whispered, "and you'll see some acrobatics that will astonish you" — which we did. Almost right away, I saw first one and then another awkward toad foot straighten out and raise up in the air, and then with a movement that would make any circus acrobat jealous, that toad gave his body a flip, and there he was right side up again.

And that was that. Warty was still alive! *Hurrah!*

I felt sorry for the other toad I had caught, though, and had brought to our garden, and tied up, and he had been swallowed by the big, ugly, hog-nosed snake; but our old favorite friend, Warty, was still alive, and that made me feel fine.

All of a sudden, Little Jim was reminded that he was supposed to hurry home with the copy of Mom's meringue pie recipe. "I've got to get going," he said. "Besides, I haven't practiced my piano lesson yet."

That little guy was certainly a grand person, I thought, as I watched him crawl through the rail fence, and run as fast as his short legs could carry him toward our front gate, with "Theodore Collins" on the mailbox beside it, scramble onto his bicycle and ride away.

I looked up at Pop, then, and said, "I'll bet you knew all the time that the toad I was trying to save wasn't Warty. You did, didn't you?"

"I'm afraid I did," Pop said. "In fact, I was watching you yesterday afternoon while you were tieing up your toad with your fishing line. After you had gone to bed last night, I went out to the garden to be sure, by taking a look at your toad's toes. I had a little trouble catching him because he was as scared of me as a cottontail rabbit. He started hopping away in short, quick jumps, almost as fast as a frog jumps, unwinding your reel a little with every jump."

And that was that, and a very exciting that, at that.

7

AUTUMN, with a million different shades of color, came to Sugar Creek. The hills that year were especially pretty after the first frost. Say, when Mom puts frosting on a pie or cake, it's nearly always one color — such as white or pink, or chocolate brown — but when old Jack Frost gets through with the maples and oaks and elms and sycamores and lindens, and a lot of other different kinds of trees on the Sugar Creek hills, they have all the colors of the rainbow at the same time.

"Did you ever see such a big bouquet of colors?" I heard Mom say to Pop one day when they were standing out by our barn looking toward Strawberry Hill.

"It is pretty, isn't it?" Pop answered her.

I don't think they knew I was behind them inside the barn looking out the open window at Strawberry Hill, myself. In fact, they didn't seem to know there was anybody in the world except themselves 'cause all of a sudden, I noticed Pop's left arm go around Mom's kind of roundish shoulders, and I heard him say, "But I like grayish-brown color just as well," — which is the color of Mom's hair.

Then Mom kind of leaned her head on Pop's big wide shoulder and said something to him which I couldn't hear, and maybe wasn't supposed to anyway. But I guess it must have been about her hair getting gray and not wanting it to 'cause Pop answered her, saying, "Everybody's life has to have a winter. That's the way God made us."

For about a whole minute, neither one of them said a word, and I was quiet as a mouse. In fact, I was even quieter 'cause right that minute, I heard a rustling noise above my head, and, looking up, I saw on the top shelf of Pop's cupboard, a pointed-nosed, beady-eyed mouse which I, knew, if Mom would see it, she'd scream like women and girls are supposed to when they see a mouse.

I kept on being quieter than a mouse, and I was glad I did, because I heard Mom say something kind of important, and it was, "I hope we can bring up our children to love the One who made those beautiful hills."

Then I saw Pop's arm tighten around Mom's shoulders. For some reason, I felt terribly good inside, and I decided I ought to try to help Mom and Pop do what they were trying to do — and were having a hard time doing.

It was time to throw down the hay for the horses, so I left the yellowish-brown-furred mouse to himself, and went over to the wooden ladder that leads up to our hayloft. When I got to the top, I started whistling, and throwing down forkfuls of sweet-smelling alfalfa, and — do you know what? — I noticed I was whistling the same hymn I had been whistling a whole lot that summer and fall, and the words of the first line were:

"A mighty fortress is our God."

All of a sudden, it seemed like He was what the song said He was, and even though He was awful wonderful, He still had time to look after me and all of our gang. In fact, I knew He was interested in us when we had that very

dangerous experience one cold winter day
that same year.

There were maybe, about three inches of
snow on the ground that day, nice fresh snow,
very white and very clean, and just right for
making tracks and snowballs, although the
weather seemed to be getting colder fast and
the snow didn't pack well into balls.

The gang had been planning to spend a
night up in the hills in the haunted house, if
our parents would let us. We had tried hard to
show them that it would be all right for us to
do it. We had carried a lot of firewood in and
stacked it in the big living room. We had even
laid the fire so it would be ready to start in
a jiffy. Also, we had cleaned the old house —
that is, the room we had planned to sleep in.
If we all took our sleeping bags and blankets
and had a good fire in the fireplace, it would
be more fun than you can shake a stick at
to stay there all night.

But our parents said we couldn't — not in
the wintertime. "Absolutely *not!*" Pop and all
the other pops had said. All of our moms had
said the same thing, only my mom had said
it first. Pop had seemed a little sad when he

had to agree with her, but he did almost right away, and that made *me* feel sad.

So it was "Absolutely *not*" for all of us. Middle-sized Jim had never been there, so we decided to take him along one day to show him the upstairs and especially the attic where we had caught the ring-tailed ghost you know about if you've read the book "The Haunted House at Sugar Creek." But there was too much snow on the ground that day for us to take Middle-sized Jim along because it'd be too hard for him to walk, even if he used his crutches; besides, it was pretty far, and he would get too tired, and none of us wanted to walk so slow as we knew we would have to if he went with us.

So we all went without him. We got into the house like we always do, through the basement first, and up through a trap door into the kitchen. Then we went upstairs where we had a lot of cold fun retelling to ourselves the exciting experiences we'd had there one dark night catching a ring-tailed ghost that had been making its home in the attic.

We even went into the attic and looked around a little. The first thing I noticed was

that a big hole which had been in the chimney
the first time we'd visited the house, had been
repaired.

" 'Tsa good thing they plugged up the
hole," Dragonfly said, "or if anybody started
a fire in the fireplace downstairs, all the
smoke'd come out here."

Along about four in the afternoon, it began to start to get dark, like it does in the wintertime, especially on a cloudy day, so we decided to get going for our different homes
which were quite a ways away.

"Let's take the shortcut home," Big Jim
said, "so we can get home in time to help our
folks do the chores." The shortcut, as you
know, is through Old Man Paddler's house
and his basement and through a long tunnel-
like cave which comes out at the other end
by the old sycamore tree. From the tree, we
would follow Sugar Creek to most of our different homes.

It didn't take us nearly as long to get back
as it had to go because we had played nearly
all the way up, like most boys do.

It hadn't been nearly as hard walking as we
thought it might be, and I was feeling kind of

sad because we hadn't taken Middle-sized Jim
along. I knew he'd feel bad about it, too, when
he found out we had gone, and hadn't even
asked him if he had wanted to go with us.

Anyway, when we got to the spring where
we had all met before we started, all of sudden Circus, who had been carrying Big Jim's
rifle, said, "Hey, gang, come here! Look!
There's some strange kind of animal been following our tracks."

His scary-sounding voice started the red
hair under my cap to moving like it was starting to start to stand straight up. We all gal-
loped through the three-inch deep snow to
where Circus was. But, shucks, I thought, it
wasn't anything. Just some kind of a human
being's tracks that had come from the direction of Circus' and Big Jim's and Middle-sized
Jim's houses.

"April fool," Circus said, when we had all
looked disgustedly down at only a boy's
tracks. "It's only a poor crippled Lion."

Well, it wasn't April the first and it didn't
seem very funny. Even though I could tell by
the tangled-up way the shoe tracks were
made, that they were Middle-sized Jim's

tracks, I didn't like anybody to call him "a poor crippled Lion." I was sure Middle-sized Jim, himself, wouldn't like it at all — he not wanting anybody to pity him, like most crippled and blind people don't, Pop says.

"Look everybody!" Poetry said with his squawky voice. "He's following our tracks! I'll bet he found out we were going on an adventure and decided to follow us! We'd better take out after him and see if we can catch up with him and stop him" — which as soon as Big Jim had thought the idea over, we all, as quick as anything, started to do.

"How long ago was he here?" Dragonfly wanted to know.

Circus, whose Pop is a hunter and trails more coons' and rabbits' tracks than any of the rest of us, stooped down and studied the tracks and said, "Maybe not more than an hour ago. Look, the wind has already filled some of the Lion's tracks with snow."

And it had. Our own tracks — the ones we had made ourselves when we had started out about two o'clock — had quite a little snow blown into them. Middle-sized Jim's tracks,

which we were sure were his because every
now and then we saw where he had used his
crutches, were a lot fresher than ours.

"Let's run," Big Jim said, "or it'll be too
dark to follow his tracks, or else maybe when
he gets to some of those places where the wind
has a clean sweep, he'll lose our trail and get
lost, and then if we can't find him, he'll have
to stay out all night in the hills and maybe
freeze to death!"

Say, that sounded like serious business. I
was thinking about the "absolute concentration" which Middle-sized Jim had to have all
the time when he walked or ran. If he got too
cold or worried or something, he might not be
able to concentrate and would have to use his
crutches. He might even fall down a lot of
times and hurt himself. He might not even be
able to get up, so if we didn't find him, he
really would be lost and have to stay out all
night in the woods in the very cold weather.

So away we all went, not stopping to think
that our own folks might be worrying about
us, wondering where we were and why we didn't
come home.

Pretty soon we came to the old sycamore tree where, earlier in the afternoon, we had decided not to go through the cave on our way to the haunted house, but instead, had gone on around the longest way. There, in the quick gathering twilight, we stopped and looked each other in our worried faces, and Big Jim said, "He's gone on, following our tracks. I was hoping he had gone into the cave, and that maybe we could follow him through and find him up in Old Man Paddler's cabin."

Little Jim, standing beside me, holding onto his ash stick, looked really concerned. I noticed his teeth were chattering with the cold, and I wished that he, being such a little guy, was home beside a nice warm fire.

"We'd better start running if we want to catch up with him, before he gets clear up to the haunted house." Big Jim studied Middlesized Jim's tracks. "At least he hasn't started falling down yet."

"Let's holler and see if we can make him hear," Circus said, he being able to make a terribly loud, high-pitched call that sounded both like a loon and a ghost. Right away, he let out a blood-curdling long, weird, high-pitched scream . . . *"Ohoooooooooooooo . . . Ohoooooooooooooo!"*

We listened, but there wasn't any answer — not even an echo — but we did *hear something*.

"Hey, what *is* that?" Dragonfly asked. "Sounds like a swarm of bees or an airplane or something."

And honest-to-goodness-for-sure, something did sound like a swarm of bees. We all listened as hard as we could, and then I began to get worried 'cause what we'd heard wasn't an airplane or a swarm of bees, but *wind* blowing through the bare branches of the oaks and maples and elms and other trees of the Sugar Creek hills.

"We've really got to get going now," Big Jim said. "That's wind! There's a terrible storm coming up, and when it hits, it'll pick up all this loose dry snow and whip it up into a blizzard! It'll cover up every track we ever made, and he'll really get lost for sure! And *we* can't follow *his* tracks either!"

Only one thing was right to do, and we started to do it, which was, hurry like a house afire on that trail, following our old tracks and Middle-sized Jim's new ones.

"It'll be dark in only a few minutes after that wind hits!" Big Jim said.

I looked toward the highest hill which was about a quarter of a mile away, and couldn't even see it because it had got dark that fast. All I could see was a whitish-dark cloud — which is the way a snowstorm looks at twilight before it reaches you.

We dived headfirst on, following the path our own feet had made in the snow, watching all the time to see if Middle-sized Jim's tracks were still following them.

But say! A thick formation of clouds was rolling across the sky, and in almost no time, it was a whirling, blinding dark, and we were in the middle of a terrible blizzard; also, at the same time, the wind struck. It seemed like the wind was acting like a giant-sized snow shovel, scooping up whole hills of snow, and socking us with it. I felt it beating against my face and neck and into my collar, and I knew we were in for some very dangerous excitement.

"H-hadn't we b-better g-g-go back h-home?" Dragonfly asked in his whining voice which he sometimes uses when he is worried. "Mother told me not to catch cold." Then he sneezed like he does when he gets ragweed or goldenrod pollen in his nose, or when he gets too close to a horse and smells its dandruffy hair.

* * *

Well, it's a queer feeling being out in the woods among the hills when a howling, blinding snowstorm is all around you, and you can't see more than a few feet in front of you or in any direction, when you know you are a long ways from home and from any kind of shelter — also when it's not only cold, but is getting colder every minute.

"We've got to find Middle-sized Jim and save him!" Big Jim gasped, and Dragonfly yelled back above the storm, holding his hand up to his mouth to keep from inhaling the cold air direct into his allergic bronchial tubes, "We've got to save ourselves!"

For once, Dragonfly was right. We all

seemed to know it at the same time. In that
blinding, madly-whirling blizzard, every direction seemed like every other direction.

"Hey, you guys!" I heard Big Jim yell.
"Come'ere! — *Quick!*"

We struggled through the snow and crowd-
ed around him in a little, gasping and panting huddle, wondering what he was going to
tell us. Also, I was looking around and down
in the snow to see if maybe he had found Middle-sized Jim.

Then in a voice that was pretty excited for
Big Jim's voice, he said, "We're lost! All our
tracks are already covered up with snow!"

It was a sickening feeling — hearing that
and knowing we really *were* lost. But Big Jim
certainly wasn't any sissy. He raised his voice
so he could be sure all of us heard him and
said, "Two things, Gang. First, we are to stick
together, so if we can't find the stone house
where we'll be sheltered from this terrible
storm, we can huddle close together and help
keep each other warm; and second, we've got
to find our directions so we'll know which way
to go."

It made sense. I knew we wouldn't have any trouble staying together, but who could tell what direction it was without any daylight or any sun — and without a compass? Every boy who spends a lot of time in the woods or anyplace where he might get lost, ought to carry a compass — which is "a small round device with a magnetic needle which always points to North."

"Any of you have a compass? Poetry, you got yours?" — Poetry sometimes carrying one with him. Also, on our hikes, Poetry always carried a waterproof match box.

Poetry tried all his pockets, and didn't have it. "I must have left it in my other pants," he said, which is what a boy does with a lot of different things when he changes clothes. I shoved my hands into my pockets, too, and pulled out a buckeye and a papaw seed, then shoved my hands back in again, and left them to keep them warm.

Well, that was that. We didn't have any compass, and there was no way of knowing what direction to go to find the old stone house. It was so blinding dark on account of the swirling, driving snow, that we couldn't see more than a half dozen white yards in front of us.

Little Jim was close beside me. I looked at his face which so much of the time is as innocent as a lamb's face, but this time it wasn't. His small jaw was set like he was getting ready to dive through a tangle of football players, and then all of surprising sudden, he said, "If we can find a *tree*, we can tell which way *north* is."

"If we can find *what?*" Circus said.

"If we can find a tree —" Little Jim was interrupted by a savage gust of wind that whipped in and cut off his breath.

As you maybe know, Little Jim was always studying nature, looking for and finding wild flowers and weeds and different kinds of trees and writing their names in his notebook. So I thought maybe he might have a bright idea. When he got his breath again, he said, "If we can find a tree, we can tell which way *north* is 'cause the thickest moss and lichen grow on the bark on the north side."

Say, as long as I have lived at Sugar Creek

where there are hundreds and hundreds of
trees, I'd never noticed that, but the minute
Little Jim said it, I knew it was true.

Also, the minute he said it, Big Jim seemed
to remember it was so — he having been a
boy scout. Right away, he said, "That's right.
Everybody hold on to everybody till we come
to a tree," which we did, and it was a white
birch tree with bark as white as snow, but had
big patches of green lichen on one side all up
and down its trunk. We studied it up close,
also several other trees near by just to be sure
that all of them had patches of lichen on the
same side, and that's how we found out which
way *north* was. But it didn't help us much,
because we still didn't know what direction
we were from the stone house. If we'd been as
well acquainted with this part of Sugar Creek
territory as we were with that section of it
which was closer to our homes, it'd have been
easy.

Circus got a bright idea then and it was,
"What direction were we going when the
storm hit while we were still following our
tracks?"

"Southwest," Big Jim said. "That old house is southwest of the sycamore tree, and we were going toward it!"

Little Jim's cheerful voice called out right then. I heard him say, "If we keep on watching the north sides of the trees, we can tell which way to keep on going!"

And so we plunged on again, going southwest, following Big Jim and Circus, who were breaking trail for us. The walking got harder and I kept stumbling over snow-covered logs and underbrush, and falling down — even worse maybe than Middle-sized Jim would have done.

I don't know what the rest of the gang was thinking about while we were struggling and gasping and plunging into and out of and through those drifts, but because I liked Middle-sized Jim very much, I kept wondering if he had managed to get to the house before the storm struck. Had he found out we weren't there and already started back on the other trail? Was he maybe lying flat in the snow somewhere unable to get up? What if we couldn't find him at all, and he would have to stay out all night? Why, he would freeze to death! It was a terribly sad thought.

Also, I was thinking something else, but I probably wouldn't have written it down for you if Little Jim hadn't been thinking the same and said it to me out loud, and this is what it was, "I wonder if Middle-sized Jim is a Christian."

I didn't know for sure. Dragonfly heard Little Jim say that, and gasped out a wheezy answer, "A Christian would freeze to death the same as anybody else, if he had to stay all night in this kind of weather." I knew Dragonfly was right because cold weather would be cold for a Christian the same as for anybody else.

It made it seem very important, though, that we find Middle-sized Jim, so without knowing I was going to do it, I yelled at the top of my lungs, calling Middle-sized Jim's name. But I could hardly hear myself. My voice sounded as dead as if I had thrown it into a lot of whirling goose feathers, on account of the roaring wind; and of course there wasn't any answer from Middle-sized Jim.

I'll have to admit I was pretty scared — for myself as well as for Middle-sized Jim. Every single member of the Sugar Creek Gang was already a Christian on account of we already shoved open the doors of our different hearts and had let the Saviour come in, and He had washed all of us from all our sins. I knew that if we had to freeze to death, we would all go straight to Heaven, but I certainly didn't want to go there that afternoon.

Even while I stumbled and plunged along behind Big Jim and some of the rest of the gang, I thought about my grayish-brown-haired Mom. I even imagined that if none of our gang came home, Pop would get up a searching party as soon as the storm was over enough so he could, and he and a lot of men would go out looking for us, and then maybe they'd find us out here in the snow, huddled together and all frozen stiff. There'd be a funeral for all of us in the Sugar Creek Church. Sylvia's pop would preach the sermon, and my pop and mom would walk slowly past the casket where their red-haired, freckled-faced boy would be lying face up — only my body would be there. My spirit would be in Heaven where all saved people's souls go the minute they die — that is, if they are *really* saved.

Say, almost before I got through imagining all that, I heard Circus, who was leading the way with Big Jim, let out a yell, saying, "Hey, gang! We're there! There's the old haunted house!"

8

THAT GREAT BIG old awkward-looking
stone house certainly looked good to me. I
was so cold and so wind-blown with powdered
snow all over me — and so also were all of
us — that it was going to be wonderful to get
inside. We would build a roaring fire in the
fireplace and all of us would get thawed out.
I almost forgot about Middle-sized Jim, but
only for a minute, 'cause when we got to the
house, we found him sprawled out by the
door, panting for breath, and as helpless as
a small wood turtle is when you turn him over
on his back in a slippery place, and he gets all
his four legs working at the same time trying
to turn back on his stomach and can't.

I tell you, we went into quick action. In
less time than it would take me to tell you
about it, we all rushed to Middle-sized Jim's
rescue and got him, along with the rest of our
very cold selves, into the basement entrance,

up through the trap door into the kitchen, and
on into a large living room where the fireplace
was, and where, in a few jiffies, we would have
a warm fire going.

It was almost dark inside, but it would be
easy to start the fire on account of when we
had been planning and hoping we could stay
all night, we had done what is called "laid the
fire," which means we had taken some straight
slivers of split sticks and some shredded bark
and made a little wigwam of them in the fireplace. Also, we had stood up some larger
pieces of wood all around them, so that all
we would have to do would be to touch a
lighted match to it. As soon as it was started
good, we'd lay larger pieces of wood on it and
also some fireplace logs which we had carried
in. Pretty soon, we'd be as warm as toast.

I couldn't help but think how maybe we'd
get to stay all night after all.

Gasping and panting and still terribly cold,
we felt our way around in the almost-dark
house.

Middle-sized Jim said, "I've got a flashlight
in my pocket, so you can see to start the fire."

"How come you got a flashlight?" Poetry's

squawky voice asked and Middle-sized Jim replied, "I keep it all the time so if I fall down somewhere outdoors at night, I can flash it on and off and my father can tell where I am."

Well, as cold as it was, and as cold as we still were, it looked like we were going to have a happy adventure. Of course, we would have to keep our fire burning all night and maybe all day tomorrow, too, until the storm stopped long enough for us to go home — or until our folks or somebody came to rescue us.

"Now, for a good warm fire," Big Jim said, walking over to a corner and leaning his already-empty .22 rifle there — Big Jim never carrying his gun loaded unless we were actually hunting. Then he turned to Poetry and said cheerfully, "O.K., fireman, let's have the matches."

Middle-sized Jim was sitting on the floor near the rifle, and Big Jim was holding the pocket flashlight on Poetry, who quick shoved one of his fat hands into his pocket for his waterproof match box.

And then, all of sickening sudden, I saw the most puzzled expression come over Poetry's face. Before any of us had time to think, he came to quick life, and in a jiffy both his hands were acting excited, and were diving in and out of first one pocket and then another. Even before he said a word, I knew he didn't have a single match.

And right that minute, it seemed like I had never been so cold in my life. The wind outside was whistling and moaning — and also howling — and snow was driving in through a crack in the window behind me. Every single one of us searched his pockets, and there wasn't a match among us — *not even one!*

Not a match among us! Zero weather! A howling blizzard and absolutely no way to start a fire!

Well, what can you do when there isn't a thing you can do? In some of the fastest remembering I had ever done, I remembered a time, one cold winter day, when we had all gone up to see Old Man Paddler in his cabin. When we got there, we found him in his cellar — he having fallen down the steps. The fire was out in the house, and there wasn't even one match to start a fire. We had saved the old man and ourselves from freezing by taking one of the lenses of his reading glasses

— which were as thick as magnifying glasses — and holding it in the sunlight just above some dry, decayed wood. The very second a little reddish spot of concentrated sunlight touched that dried, decayed wood, there was smoke. Big Jim had kept on holding it there, blowing his breath on it at the same time until there was a reddish glow in the punk — which is the name for that kind of dried, decayed wood. The little glow grew bigger and brighter as Big Jim kept on blowing his breath on it, moving the spot of light around a little so the fire would spread. Then he took a piece of rolled-up tissue paper, touched it to the live coal, blowing his breath on it at the same time, and — presto-chango — just like that — all of a sudden, there was a flame of fire! Only a few jiffies later, we had had a roaring fire in the old man's fireplace.

But there wasn't any sunlight in an old stone house in the middle of a Sugar Creek blizzard.

"We could start a fire by friction like Indians do, if we had a bow and arrow," Dragonfly said, his voice sounding like his teeth were chattering from the cold.

Big Jim turned the idea over in his mind. But we didn't have any bow, and even if we had had, the thong would have to be made out of leather, and we didn't have any; although, maybe we could have cut a long strip of leather from one of our belts. We would also need what is called a *soapstone,* which we didn't have. Even if any of us had known for sure how to start a fire by friction, we didn't have the material with which to do it with us anyway.

It was still not quite dark in the house, on account of the white snow outside, so we could see each other's face a little even when we didn't have the flashlight turned on.

"Are there any blankets anywhere?" Middle-sized Jim asked, his voice trembling. I noticed he was shivering pitifully. He was probably colder than any of the rest of us because we had been running and fighting against the storm right up until the last minute, while he had only been lying helpless outside the door without being able to get up. I guess I never felt so sorry for a person in my life as I did for that good-hearted, spastic boy. I knew there weren't any blankets, and I hated to have to tell him, but I did, and sat down beside him to help him get warm.

Little red-haired Tom Till spoke up and said, "Maybe some of our folks will come for us."

"Not tonight — they won't," Poetry said. "Nobody could walk in this wind."

We didn't want to use up all the battery in Middle-sized Jim's flashlight, so we turned it off and stared at each other in the light-dark. I felt myself shivering and shivering. We huddled close together and listened to the wind howling and moaning and the snow beating against the windows.

"We'd better keep moving," Big Jim said, "or we'll freeze."

It was a good idea, only of course Middle-sized Jim couldn't walk very well and he couldn't swing his arms around and beat them against his sides like the rest of us could.

All the time, time was passing. The wind sounded like a lot of angry wild animals; and the snow, beating against the windows, sounded like somebody was out there throwing sand against them, and I began to feel desperate.

We couldn't go home, and we didn't have a match or a thing to start a fire with.

"Looks like we're going to get to do what we wanted to do," Big Jim said, but he didn't say it very cheerfully.

It certainly wasn't a happy prospect 'cause if there is anything in the world that makes you feel discouraged, it is to be too cold and not have any way to get warm.

"There ought to be just one match around here, somewhere," Big Jim said; and all of us went through all our pockets again to look. I went through all thirteen of mine — four in my trousers, four in my overalls which were over my trousers, four in my mackinaw, and one in my shirt. In almost less than no time, all eight of us had searched all of our nearly one hundred pockets and there wasn't a match among us. If we had emptied out all the stuff we had, it'd have made a big pile; there being such things as coins, buckeyes, papaw seeds, knives, nails, nuts and bolts, pieces of string, watches, pencils, fountain pens, and other stuff that boys always carry — enough maybe to start a secondhand store in Sugar Creek.

I noticed Big Jim had a small box of .22 caliber cartridges for his rifle. Little Jim and three or four of the rest of us had our small, thin, leather New Testaments. Seeing mine, I was reminded that there was a God, and that maybe if nobody among us could do anything about getting a fire started, He could show us what to do. I knew if Sylvia's pop had been there, he would probably ask us to bow our heads and shut our eyes, and he'd say, like he sometimes does at church, "Let us all pray." I also thought that since God had made the world and all the boys in it, He might answer prayer and help us get a fire started so we could get warm — but Sylvia's pop wasn't there.

Most of us put our stuff back in our pockets, except Little Jim who, I noticed, kept his New Testament out, holding it half hidden in one of his hands.

I got a fine surprise, though, when Big Jim said in a voice that sounded like he was almost angry, "Do we all claim to be Christians, or don't we?"

Not a one of us answered him, but I felt myself swallowing something in my throat. I glanced down at Little Jim's New Testament, and noticed that he was holding on to it terribly tight. Then Big Jim said, "If any of our dads was here, we'd ask him if he had a match, or if he could help us start a fire, wouldn't we?"

Still not a one of us answered a word. Big Jim spoke again in a firm voice, "All right, then, our dads aren't here, but we all know Who is . . . Everybody bow his head, shut his eyes, and keep still. Let each one make his own silent prayer."

Quick as anything, all our heads went down. I didn't know I had my cap off, even as cold as it was, until I felt it in my hands, then I remembered that that is what you are supposed to do when you pray.

I guess I didn't say much of a prayer except to ask God to do anything He could about the Sugar Creek Gang, and especially Middle-sized Jim who was sort of leaning against me and shaking with the cold.

I didn't suppose any of us would pray out loud — although, at the Sugar Creek Church, when we have what is called Bible Treasure Club, different ones of us sometimes did, even though we were as bashful as anything about doing it — but a jiffy later, I heard Big Jim's voice and he was making as nice a prayer as anybody in the church could have made. Part of it was, ". . . We're just a bunch of worried boys who have to have help and we know You can do anything. If there is any way we can help ourselves, please show us what it is, and we'll try to do it . . . . Bless our folks and help them not to worry, but it does look like we'll have to have a fire or we'll freeze."

The word "freeze" seemed to make me shiver a little harder than I had been.

Big Jim hadn't any sooner finished his prayer, than Dragonfly spoke up with what sounded like the absolutely dumbest thing he had ever said in his life, and it was, "Whyn't we do like the Indians do and make a smoke signal for our folks to see, and then —"

That was as far as Dragonfly got. Circus interrupted saying, "You're crazy! How can you get smoke without a fire? That's what we have to have — a *fire!*"

"I was trying to be funny," Dragonfly said, and Circus said, "You didn't try hard enough.

But if you'd try being crazy once, you wouldn't have to try so hard."

Anyway, the very minute Dragonfly mentioned smoke, Little Jim spoke up and said, "You could get a *little* smoke if you would shoot Big Jim's rifle." Then like he knew his idea wasn't any good, he added, "But nobody would see it."

Say, the very minute Little Jim said what he said, Big Jim jumped like he had been shot at and hit. He looked quick at Middle-sized Jim and exclaimed, "That book on outdoor life you let me read last summer — wasn't there something in it about starting a fire — you know — like lost hunters do sometimes when they haven't any matches?"

"That's too dangerous for a boy," Middle-sized Jim said, and his voice was trembling and he was actually shaking with the cold.

Big Jim's face was set grimly, and it seemed like he was feeling responsible for all of us — he being the leader. "It wouldn't be as dangerous as freezing to death," he said.

"What wouldn't?" I thought, but didn't say so.

And then I heard Big Jim mumbling as if to himself, as he beat his mittened hands together to keep the circulation going. A jiffy later, he said, "I've got to do it — danger or no danger!" Then he raised his voice and said to all of us, "There's only one way to start a fire, and it's very dangerous!"

Just as he finished saying it, there was a banging noise upstairs or on the roof or somewhere, like a branch of a tree had broken off in the wind and fallen on the house. That noise seemed to help Big Jim to make up his mind, 'cause right away he started doing things, "Here goes," he said almost savagely. He quick shoved one of his hands into one of his pockets and pulled out his box of .22 caliber cartridges, and a jiffy later he had one of them in his cold, shivering hand.

"Be *careful!*" Dragonfly exclaimed excitedly. "It might go off!"

"I know it," Big Jim answered, "but I don't think it will if I am careful. You guys step back — all but Circus. Circus, you hold the flashlight for me."

All of us got back a few feet. With both my cold, worried eyes, I watched Big Jim. I could see the muscles of his jaw working, and his face was tense. His fuzzy upper lip seemed to be trembling, and maybe his teeth were chattering, too; and I knew it wasn't because of the cold weather, but, was because what he was going to do was very dangerous.

Circus' hand that was holding the small flashlight was trembling, too. I noticed that part of the flashlight's beam went on past the small, copper cartridge Big Jim was holding, and lighted up the fireplace which had in it the shredded bark and fine wood shavings, as well as the larger pieces of wood. Big Jim's hands were almost fiery red with cold, and they were so numb that he was having a hard time doing what he wanted to do with the cartridge. "Here," he said. "Hold it a minute, while I get my hands warm."

He laid the cartridge in Circus' palm, straightened up, stepped toward the center of the room, shoved his hands back into his mittens, and began swinging his hands round and round his body and beating them together to get the blood to circulating again. Then he quick took off his mittens and taking the small copper cartridge in his fingers, he started working and worrying at the lead bullet in it, twisting carefully and pulling, until all of a sudden the bullet came out, and he had the shell with the powder in it in one hand and the bullet in the other.

"Here, Bill," he said, "hold this bullet," handing it to me.

I took the lead bullet in my hand, knowing that by itself it wasn't dangerous to hold, not any more than if I'd found a piece of lead along Sugar Creek.

The next thing Big Jim did was to very carefully pour out most of the black powder from the shell — being extra careful not to spill any of it, but pouring it out on the window sill on the opposite side of the room from the fireplace. In fact, he poured it into a little patch of powdered snow. "It'll get wet in the snow," he said, "and won't be dangerous. After we get the fire started in the fireplace, we'll throw it out into the storm."

What he was doing still didn't make sense because I couldn't see how in the world he could get a fire started that way. But he acted like he knew what he was doing, while the rest of us, except Circus, stayed where we were and watched — and maybe helped a little by praying — although I didn't feel like I was a good enough boy for God to answer, even if I was a Christian.

I kept thinking that the powder was easily ignited and very dangerous, and I was glad Big Jim was being very careful, 'cause if that powder exploded in his hands it might give him a terribly bad powder burn. It might even put out his eyes, like firecrackers do when they explode in a boy's hands too close to his eyes. Of course, we had all fired firecrackers on the Fourth of July, but that was different. They had fuses on them, and none of us were ever close to them when they exploded.

"Now," Big Jim said, "who wants to sacrifice a small strip of his cotton shirttail? It's got to be cotton."

"*I* don't," Dragonfly said. "Mother would give me a lickin' if anybody cut a hole in my shirt."

"Here's mine," Little Jim said, and he already had his coat unbuttoned and his shirt tail out in front, and Big Jim ordered Poetry, "You snip off a very small strip and make it into a wad the size of a small garden pea."

It still didn't make sense. How could any-body start a fire with a practically empty shell and a piece of a boy's shirt tail?

Quicker'n anything Poetry had his scout knife out, and a piece of Little Jim's green-and-white-striped shirttail cut off and wadded into a small wad. Very carefully then, Big Jim plugged that very small, pea-sized piece of cotton shirt tail into the end of the cartridge where the bullet had been.

Then I saw Big Jim's jaw set firmly as he straightened up and said, "Now we're ready. Hand me the rifle."

His rifle, as you know, was leaning against the wall in the corner, and was already empty on account of, as I've already told you, Big Jim knew how to be careful with a gun, that being one of the reasons his folks let him own one.

Quicker'n anything he had the gun loaded with the shirttail bullet.

"You goin' to *shoot* a fire into the fireplace?" Dragonfly asked.

Hearing that, the whole idea began to make sense to me.

"No," Big Jim answered Dragonfly. "The

smoke and the force of the wind might blow our shredded bark away. I've got a better idea."

The next few jiffies were the most interesting ones I'd had in a long time, although I was shivering with the cold and worrying as much as I could — and maybe I was praying a little bit, too.

"Attention, everybody," Big Jim ordered. "I'm going to shoot this cotton bullet straight toward the ceiling. It can't start a fire up there because the ceiling is plaster. But the cotton bullet *will* come down in the room here somewhere, and it will be smoldering, like a firecracker does after it has gone off. Don't anybody touch it; I'll take care of it."

I could feel my heart pounding fast as he held the gun with the muzzle toward the dark ceiling. "Watch it now!" Big Jim said grimly.

Dragonfly, beside me, grabbed his nose because the smell of smoking gun powder always made him sneeze.

Then as quick as anything, when Big Jim pulled the trigger, I saw a spit of flame shoot up into the air out of the rifle's muzzle, and at the same time Little Jim's piece of shirttail flew up to the ceiling, and a second later it plopped down smoldering right close to Poetry. Big Jim pounced upon it, whisked it up in his leather-palmed mitten, dashed to the fireplace with it and laid it right in the center of the dry tinder. In terribly fast time, he was down on his knees, holding the flashlight on the little pile of tinder with the smoking piece of Little Jim's shirt tail in the center of it, and was blowing his breath on it.

And say! What to my wondering eyes should appear but a little yellow flame shooting up from the tinder! Then there were more flames, and bigger ones, and I began to hear a very cheerful crackling noise like a live fire always makes, and I knew our lives were saved.

We knew we would have to stay in the house all night — or most of it anyway — so as soon as we got warm, we began to have fun talking it all over and even laughing about it. Middle-sized Jim had certainly turned out to be a very interesting boy to have with us. In fact if he hadn't followed our trail, we wouldn't have followed his, and we wouldn't have got to stay all night in the haunted house like we had wanted to do in the first place.

After we got completely thawed out Big Jim said to us, as he sat on the floor with the firelight flickering on his fuzzy upper lip, "I guess we owe a vote of thanks to Somebody, don't we?"

When he said "Somebody," the serious way he said it, made me know *Whom* he meant, and it also made me feel good inside. Right away my thoughts jumped clear over the tops of the blizzard-swept hills clear back to the Sugar Creek Church where we all went every Sunday, and which is how we happened to believe in God in the first place.

My thoughts were interrupted when Poetry spoke up and said, "What's that song you're whistling, Bill?"

Say, it was just like it had been that other day in the summertime when I had been whistling without knowing it. I thought a jiffy, and part of the tune was still in my mind, and it was the same one I'd been whistling a lot of times that summer and fall and winter.

I knew Poetry knew the name of the song

so I wasn't going to tell him, but I wouldn't have needed to anyway, 'cause all of a friendly sudden, Middle-sized Jim answered me saying, "That's Martin Luther's famous hymn, *A Mighty Fortress is Our God.* He wrote it over four hundred years ago, after he had been reading the Forty-sixth Psalm in the Bible. The first line of it is on the tombstone in Germany where he is buried — I read it in a book my folks gave me when I became a Christian."

Hearing him say that, made me look quick at Little Jim, just as he looked quick at me. Little Jim took a deep breath and sighed and I thought his mouse-like face looked like he was very glad inside.

In fact, I felt fine myself, on account of the wonderful way everything had turned out. As I sat with the cold air pushing against my back and with the fire pushing its very friendly heat against my face, it seemed like there was a warm feeling in my heart toward God, not only 'cause He had saved our lives but because He really liked me, and it didn't make any difference about Middle-sized Jim's being a spastic — He liked him just as much as if he were a boy with a perfect body.

Dragonfly spoke up then, and said — sneezing just before he said it — "My folks might take me down South after Christmas, and let me go to school down there where I won't get so many colds and sneeze so much, and have to miss so much school."

I looked at his kinda pinched face, and wished he didn't have to stay up North in the cold Sugar Creek winter. In fact, I'd kinda like to go to a warm climate myself, I thought; and *say!* — just like that! — I began to hope that if Dragonfly's parents decided to take him down to Texas or Arizona or somewhere for a month or two during the coldest part of the winter, maybe some of our parents would let us go, too, even if we couldn't stay.

Boy oh, boy, it would be wonderful! Why, down South, they not only had warm weather in the winter, but there were a million things for a boy to see and do! If you went far enough, you could go fishing in the Gulf of Mexico and catch a fish as big as a boy. . . .

If Dragonfly *does* go and any of the rest of us get to go along, I'll tell you about it. Imagine catching a fish as big as a boy!

THE END

Moody Press, a ministry of the Moody Bible Institute, is designed for education, evangelization and edification. If we may assist you in knowing more about Christ and the Christian life, please write us without obligation to: Moody Press, c/o MLM, Chicago, Illinois 60610.